THE
HIDDEN
APARTMENT
AND
OTHER STORIES

BROOKE FIELDHOUSE

Matador
9 Priory Business Park,
Wistow Road, Kibworth Beauchamp,
Leicestershire. LE8 0RX
Tel: 0116 279 2299
Email: books@troubador.co.uk
Web: www.troubador.co.uk/matador
Twitter: @matadorbooks

ISBN 978 1838595 173

British Library Cataloguing in Publication Data.
A catalogue record for this book is available from the British Library.

Printed and bound by CPI Group (UK) Ltd, Croydon, CR0 4YY
Typeset in 11pt Adobe Garamond Pro by Troubador Publishing Ltd, Leicester, UK

Matador is an imprint of Troubador Publishing Ltd

"The questions of the world are hidden forever, but the answers in a book are hiding in plain sight."
Lemony Snicket

"Man is not what he thinks he is, he is what he hides."
Andre Malraux

ACKNOWLEDGEMENTS

THE ART OF OWNERSHIP was first published by Fiction on the Web in Sept 2015

OPEN HOUSE was first published by Fiction on the Web in Oct 2016

THE MAGIC CARPET was first published by Fiction on the Web in July 2017

ALL PHOTO IMAGES by Gareth Buddo @furmoto except p. 73, which was taken by the author.

CONTENTS

OPEN HOUSE

'...ast year one of the guests rifled through my wife's drawers, would you believe?' announces Fractal to the group awaiting a tour of his minimalist apartment.

'Oooooh… Hope she wasn't wearing them at the time!'

Fractal's eyebrows arch; his head swivels towards the voice. He doesn't like the sound of that… Not at all.

Visitors are gathering at the white entrance door, feet tapping the white floor… Eyes roving the white shininess of walls, white ceiling, white furniture, *everything* is white.

Bald heads gleam as sunlight streams through the window; stubbly beards look suitably pointillist. Clothing is black, and there's an air of dedication.

Fractal can see a man with a long rubbery neck, pale ice-cream-cone hair, and a navy club blazer – emblazoned breast pocket. Under the man's chin, he can make out the swirl of red paisley. There's more than a touch of, *nudge nudge, wink wink, say-no-more*, about this guy. Fractal is going to have to keep an eye on him.

It was the third year he'd taken part in Open House…
Couldn't resist it. The exalted praise, the tributes, looks
of reverence on the faces of the design-faithful… Yes, 8a
Kensington Terrace was well on its way to becoming a
shrine. Every August when particulars were posted online,
he felt a thrill: '*The ultimate London apartment conversion…
architecture brought to shining, sliding life; sheer mechanical
ballet.*'

It was all worth it – even the drawer-rifling incident.
Out of two hundred and fifty visitors, you were bound to
get the odd weirdo.

Fractal has got Kubrick's *2001: A Space Odyssey* playing
on the giant HD screen, he can see heads nodding, hear
murmurs of approval… Final words of introduction, hand
raised – as if in benediction – and the group follows him
noiselessly over poured-rubber floors, past the dining alcove,
food prep area, and the bar where people pause and perch on
iridescent swivel chairs.

'Mr Rubberneck' seems to be saying something to two
tall, slender females; their hair tied Roman-style, one blonde,
the other brunette; one silver-clad, the other sheathed in
gold. Fractal catches the words, '…*end of the rainbow, end
of the rainbow!*'

Folk are spilling into bedrooms, stroking sensor showers,
worrying over waste-disposal systems, and peering into the
anti-gravity toilet. Others luxuriate on soft-touch, stain-free
fabrics, enjoying the LEDs noiselessly playing their way
through the spectrum; cerise, gold, mint, aqua, indigo; back
to cerise.

'Mmmmm, suits *you*, sir!'

Fractal is appalled to see Rubberneck fingering the black wool Nehru collar worn by another of the male guests. The man recoils, swishes his pigtail, and tugs on his sandalwood-oiled beard.

'No offence, no offence.' Rubberneck's hands touch as if in homily. This guy really doesn't fit; what's he doing here?

Visitors marvel at the winter garden. Here grows sapodilla, flaming sword, and luscious-leafed Hawaiian Ti plant. There's ylang-ylang, and glimpses of an aku aku figurine. The system is hacked to create a simulated thunderstorm every fifteen minutes. Guests have difficulty in naming plants.

'Phone a friend, phone a friend!' chants Rubberneck.

The garden *was* exquisite. Fractal had to thank Cassie for that – Cassandra she was, really. She'd made a project of it when the twins were six. That was two years ago, and Joe and Luke had loved every minute of it.

'Better than the Eden Project!' somebody purrs. 'Essence of Nick Grimshaw.'

'Lovely jubbly,' slobbers Rubberneck.

'Aponogeton!' exclaims one of the guests – remembering a plant name.

'Boom boom!' booms Rubberneck.

'Come on, Jimbo!' says the girl in gold throatily, as she and her silver friend loop arms through the sleeves of the club blazer and steer him towards the entrance door.

So, it's goodnight from him! Fractal breathes a sigh… He doesn't want anybody called Jimbo on *his* property.

3

'…Nice to see you, to see you nice!' Fractal can hear them climbing the Area steps outside the apartment. He was just a friendly mug; there was bound to be one.

Later, Fractal takes his car to get petrol – early start for a business trip to Norwich. As he drives down Kensington Terrace, he can't help noticing a man standing under the sodium light, staring at the apartment… can't help seeing the cone of pale hair, the badge of the club blazer, and the swirl of paisley around the neck.

Because he can't see him when he returns, Fractal assumes the man has gone – that is, until he gets up to pee at 4.00am and notices that the figure is still there.

£4.1 million! Not bad for a four-bed basement apartment. Fractal had it valued every year… And he hadn't paid a penny for it.

The even crazier thing was that Dad hadn't paid a *brass razu* for it either… Came back from travelling in Nepal, found it – *dero*, squatted there with friends – whole house, all six floors… Had a floor each – grew shit in the loft. Dad invented a solar heating system, had the place wrapped in silver foil. Fractal had photos… looked like Andy Warhol's Factory.

'Adverse Possession', Dad called it – that was the legal term. He said it was something that had been around since the philosopher John Locke. It was all about 'rights'; you just had to know how to exploit the system.

Then Mum died, just like that – cerebral haemorrhage. Dad announced that he was going to 'retire' – sell up and move to California – but before he put the house on the market, he got separate deeds for the basement, and made a

4

gift of it to Fractal. It was more than Fractal felt he deserved… he knew he'd been a disappointment to the old man.

Two years later, Dad was dead. It was true what they said about a broken heart.

'*So how was Open House?*' The curiosity in Tonal's voice sounded potent as it resounded over the in-car technics. Fractal was driving south on the M11, had left the house at 6.00am to look at farmland near Norwich… A housing development. How he hated that work, but it was bread and butter.

'Goooood…' Fractal could feel a mild irritation at the back of his neck. 'Good,' he repeated, scratching hard with left hand. 'Good attendance… except, Cassie thinks we should call it a day after this one.'

'…*Don't blame her, rather you than me.*'

Fractal had never told Tonal about the apartment – about Dad and the house. Lots of people had hippie parents, and you didn't have to share *all* your thoughts with friends. Funny how you hold back with friends – find yourself opening up to strangers. Cassie said that was a bad trait, and she knew all right, because she knew more about Fractal than any other living person, even if there *were* lots of things that he didn't tell her. Cassie and the twins; they were all Fractal had got.

It's early evening when Fractal arrives back at Kensington Terrace. He eases the car past lanky poplars, overhanging laurels; window down. He can smell freshly mown grass… can see something in the air above the communal garden. It looks like an insect, a large dragonfly, colourful and

hovering. He can hear the shouts of children, see Joe and Luke jumping, running clockwise in a circle, while the dragonfly seems to be winking with tiny lights; mint and cerise. At the centre of the circle stands a man holding what appears to be a black remote control. The man has a long neck, is wearing a club blazer, and just below his chin Fractal can see the swirl of red paisley.

What the hell is Rubberneck doing with *his* kids? He will go straight over and tell him to sod off! But he can hear a small voice inside him urging him to caution as he parks in his usual space, locks, tiptoes across, and peeps through the laurels. It's a drone, a tiny drone, and Fractal watches as Joe and Luke bounce up and down trying to touch it, while the man manoeuvres it just out of their reach. He will ask Cassie.

'Who, Jim...?' She made it sound as if Fractal was missing a trick.

'Jim?' Fractal felt stupid, angry, but he could feel the flesh on his buttocks beginning to creep. How did Cassie know him?

'Jim who... and what the hell's he doing?'

'It's okay, Fraaact, he came over to check it was all right, and Dan's there with Emmaaa... he's notta paedo or anything. Anyway, he's a friend of *yours* – isn't he?'

'Not exactly...'

'He says he was here on Saturday.'

'He was. I forgot to mention it.' Fractal wished he had. Cassie would have been on her guard. He would go over, get rid of Jim, and that would be the end of the matter.

'Fract? Just try and chill, will you? Everything's fiiiine!'

Fractal races up the Area steps onto the street, pads across in his espadrilles, pauses to pull out his key for the garden gate. He can feel his heart quicken.

He moves across the grass towards the man, holding out his right hand in front of him, ready to greet.

'Good game, good game!' he can hear the man shouting.

'Good game, good game!' echo Joe and Luke – ignoring Fractal.

As Fractal gets within a yard of him, the man turns his back, while the boys keep leaping and capering. Fractal dithers. Baggy, grey tee furled over putty-coloured chinos, his espadrilles soaking up moisture from the grass. The man is wearing smart, stout brown brogues.

'Thank you for looking after my children.' Fractal's voice sounds reedy, like a damaged wind instrument. No response. 'I said, thank you for looking after my children, we have to go now.'

'All right, keep your hair on, Grandad!'

The man swings round to face Fractal, teeth cemented into the rictus of a stand-up comic.

'Keep your hair on, Grandad,' parrot the twins.

'Come on, boys. I'm making supper. Remember I said I'd show you how to make a Caesar salad?'

'Ooo, render unto Caesar what is due to Caesar, eh? Game over, fun over, game over, fun over…' Fractal feels boring, spoil-sportish, but he needs to break the spell of this sinister pied piper.

He takes Joe's left hand, grasps Luke's right and – trying not to hurry – walks towards the gate. His buttocks are tingling inside his cotton boxers. He locks the garden gate behind him and wonders how the man got in there.

'…So, I lent him my key; so, he forgot to give it you back. It's not as if he's got the key to the house. Chill out, Fract, you're not going to wake up and find him standing at the end of our bed!'

'I don't like the guy.'

'Well, according to you, you don't even know him. Remember, *you* invited him here.'

'I didn't.'

'*Oh* yes you did. Think about it, Fract.'

'*Oh* yes you did, *oh* no you didn't,' parodied the twins, po-going up and down, eyes luminous, faces crimson.

'Anyway, he mentioned something about Tonal… knew you'd been to look at Lambs Farm at Norwich.'

This time Fractal could feel the flesh on his entire body creeping, and his pelvis felt strangely numb.

Back at the office, Fractal had meant to find out what was going on. Tonal must have been talking to Cassie. Fractal hadn't told her any details about the Lambs Farm deal. But there was a lot happening; Tonal was pressing forward with plans for a merger… not *exactly* merger – more buy-out. '…Make us money,' Tonal insisted. 'About time we did!' There were lots of things Fractal had *meant* to tell Tonal and hadn't, and now didn't seem the time to start worrying him with that weirdo.

'*Jim's coming round at five.*' Cassie's voice sounded excited on the mobile.

'Jim who?'

'*You know – the guy who helped me out with Joe and Luke… the drone man?*' Fractal felt a twinge of something.

'…*He's got tickets for the science museum event; the one you were going to take the twins to but you can't because you've got a buy-out meeting with Tonal. Isn't that right?*'

She was baiting him, ever so slightly – was making it sound as if she had no alternative, as if she was being forced to let the kids go with Jim.

'I don't trust the guy. He could be a stalker.'

'*If he's a stalker, love, it's you who he's stalking, not me! Look, we'll be back by 8.00… everything'll be fiiine!*'

It wasn't the fact that they were all going and *he* wasn't that was making Fractal edgy; it was that guy, Jim.

'…*You're not jealous, are you?*' Her voice had a flirtatious giggle to it.

'…Of course not…'

'…*Well, you should be!*' It was a joke.

He rang off… hit the *Cassie* button again as he thought of something else.

'How did you arrange all this… I mean, did he telephone you, call at the house?'

'*Oh… I ran into him outside my office. It was lunchtime, he suggested we have a bite, it seemed churlish to refuse…*'

'Yes, of course.'

'*Fraaact, just stay cool, will you. There's nothing in it. Stop being paranoid, he only wants to help… Luv ya!*' She'd gone.

The buy-out meeting seemed to go on forever, and it was 10.00pm before Fractal got back.

Before he opens the door, Fractal peers through the window, can see that Jim is still there. Club blazer contemptuously hanging over the edge of the white leather banquette, paisley-necked figure stretched insolently, left hand balancing wine goblet – right little finger indecently circling its rim.

Fuck you, mate! Fractal closes the door behind him noisily.

'Ooo, shut that door, shut that door!' lampoons Jim, swings his grey-worsted trousered legs together, and raises his left hand.

'Hello, love!' shouts Fractal over Jim's head; tries to ignore, struggles to sound confident, but his voice seems oddly shrill. Cassie appears from the multi-coloured glow of the bar, smiling. She is wearing silver slim-cut jeans, and a matching top showing two inches of bare midriff. She looks fantastic, but Chriiist!

'Hello, love, Jimbo stayed for some supper.'

Oh, so it's *Jimbo* now, is it? Well, sod you, Jimbo. Fractal will deal with this right now. He embraces Cassie, turns to the man.

'Jim, I can't thank you enough for what you've done for the boys… look, something's come up at work and I urgently need to be alone with my wife, so if you wouldn't mind…' Fractal takes the wine glass from Jim's hand, places it ringingly on the white table top, lifts the blazer and holds it up to the man's shoulders as he rises from the banquette. This guy has to go, for good.

'No offence, no offence.' Jim's hands move together in homily.

'Thankseverso, Jimbo.' Cassie holds her hand towards Jim and gives him a chinny sort of smile.

'Not at all, pleasure all mine, how tickled I ham, missus!' Jim leans forward, fondles her fingers; kisses them noisily.

'See you next week!'

Not bloody likely.

Fractal steers Jim through the front door, closes it behind him, and feels his fingers pushing at the man's worsted left elbow. He can hear brown brogues stamping grittily up the Area steps and onto the pavement.

Fractal is starving hungry. The others at the meeting all ate, but he had to go into a half-hour phone conversation with the Lambs Farm client and missed his chance. He's tired, his head aches, and he can feel his heart beating like a bongo.

'All's fair in love and war, all's fair in love and war.' What the *hell* does he mean by that? Fractal urges the man further down the terrace so that the two of them are clear of the front window.

'Look, I don't quite know how to say this. I don't wish to offend you, but I can't think of any way of saying it other than I don't want you coming here again. I don't want you seeing my children, and I want you to stay away from my wife.' There, he's said it.

The man says nothing, looks away from him. His limbs seem to go limp, as if his feet have been lifted off the pavement, and his body is dangling on invisible ropes. Shit! But he couldn't have done it differently. The man's head is still turned away, apparently looking towards the garden. Fractal is standing next to him, and for a moment he's worried that the man is going to crumple and collapse at his feet.

Without warning and with incomprehensible force, the man swings round and brings his clenched fist into Fractal's stomach. Fractal's head goes back, can feel his top jaw lifting as his lungs try to pull in air that doesn't exist.

He falls forward, knuckles and fingers scraping cement flags as he fights to support his body. His arms and legs seem to set like aggregate, and for a period which he is incapable of measuring, he remains, forehead touching concrete. By the time he has prised his limbs into a standing position, he notices he is alone in the street.

As Fractal sat on the Area steps, he was relieved that Cassie did not come out to look for him. It would give him time to recover. He would tell her that he and Jim had been for a walk. He could not bear to tell her the truth.

Fractal was glad it was the summer holidays. Joe and Luke had gone to stay with Cassie's mum. Not that he wanted to be away from them – on the contrary – but there were things on his mind. The Jim thing had shaken him up. Nobody had ever been violent towards him. Cassie knew something was up, had tried to get it out of him, but he wouldn't give. What would have been the point? The incident was barely credible, why should she believe him? *She* couldn't see any harm in Jim, and even if he'd convinced her that Jim was sinister, she'd say it was all Fractal's fault: '*You* encouraged him, love!'

There was something else troubling Fractal. Cassie had said that all he had to do was tell the doctor, but he couldn't bring himself to mention it; it made him feel inadequate. 'Lots of blokes get it, Fractal; just chill, will you… He'll probably just prescribe Viagra.'

Cassie had gone to see her old friend Sigrid in Kingston… Girls' night out. She was late; it was past one in the morning.
    '*…I've had too much to drink… I'm staying over.*'

IMPORTANT. This installation or part of it is
protected by a fuse/cb which automatically switches off our
supply, if an earth fault develops, find quickly by pressing
the button marked "T" or "Test". The device should switch off
the supply, if it does not, it must be serviced at ....

'Yes, of course.' Fractal, *so* accommodating!

'...*Luv ya!*

On impulse, he telephoned Sigrid's landline... No reply.

He was seized with an old and familiar insecurity. His stomach clenched as if he'd ingested some drug; his saliva became tangy. He put the apartment onto automatic, slammed, locked, and raced up the Area steps, still wearing his espadrilles.

The drive to Kingston took him over half an hour. He parked outside Sigrid's house, pussy-footed up and down the street. Cassie's car was nowhere to be seen. Of course it wasn't... because she wasn't there! Because she'd planned all this; the kids safely away at Gran's, Fractal placated, tucked up for the night – '*Luv ya!*

She was with Jim, she had to be... No doubt about it; her whole attitude, demeaning, diminishing, devaluing his feelings. '*Chill out, Fract, everything'll be fiiine, you're over-reacting; you're being sooo strraight...*'

When he got back, he scribbled a note: '*Gone away for a few days to think things out.*' It was clumsy, but it would let her know that he knew what she was up to – that he was no fool. It was coded, of course. The wording implied that *he* would be doing the thinking, but the reality was that he was giving *her* an interlude in which to think. He packed wheeled luggage, and before 8.00 he was out of the apartment and booking into a Premier Inn. He left his stuff there and went into work.

All morning he could feel the mobile vibrating in his pocket.

'Cassie'sbeenonthelandlineagaaaiin,' chanted Unproductive Andrea. 'Didn't you call'erbaack?'

Leave it, let her stew. He'd meant to tell Tonal about what was happening, but the office had gone crazy. Three new projects had come in – courtesy of the prospective management. Things were looking up.

Fractal had thought he'd be back home by the end of the week, but it wasn't working out. After a day and a half, the telephone calls stopped. He called Cassie; no reply. The boys would be back tomorrow, ready for the start of autumn term. He rang Cassie's mum. 'I don't want to take sides.' She was right, of course. He would go round, call at the house after work.

It was dark by the time he clicked his way through the front gate and tiptoed down the Area steps. He hesitated before putting the key in the door, peered through the front window. My God!

His beautiful, white, poured-rubber floor was littered with CD covers and computer game boxes. Some of the touch-latch secret cupboard doors were hanging open, stuff spewing onto the floor, and he could see a dark-red stain on the white leather banquette. *They* were sitting there – Joe, Luke, and Cassie – watching the eviction from the *Big Brother* house on *his* HD screen. Cassie was wearing a pair of leopard-skin print dungarees!

Fractal let out a sob and moved to the front door, fumbling for his key. It would only take half an hour to clear everything up. Then they could all get back to normal. But his key wouldn't fit, and when he returned to the window to tap on the glass, he found himself staring at the white wood panels of closed shutters.

He tried ringing the bell, knocking softly; Cassie's mobile, the landline. Then he climbed up the Area steps and shambled back down Kensington Terrace. He would have to find a flat; he couldn't stay at the Premier for ever.

He took a studio flat in a big, square block built from bright orange brick, just off Goldhawk Road. It wouldn't be for too long – he'd find a way of talking to Cassie. His bank account was overdrawn and he was subsisting on the 'peanuts' he and Tonal paid themselves – but things would change, after the buy-out. He'd given up his plan to tell Tonal about him and Cassie… but surely the two of them were in contact; why didn't Tonal say anything?

Fractal tried writing, no reply… Went round to Cassie's office but she was 'out with a client'. He'd heard that people often went to solicitors, but he'd never intended anything to be as serious as that.

He visited the apartment every evening; stood in the street, watching and waiting. Sometimes he slunk down the Area steps and squinted through the window. Cassie and the twins would be watching *Come Dine with Me*, the boys aping the antics of the contestants. Cassie had dyed her lovely brunette hair silver blonde, with pink and blue streaks.

Whenever he rang the bell or knocked, nobody seemed to hear. He considered lying in wait, waylaying the children and kidnapping them. But that was crazy, as mad as what he'd done by flouncing off like that in the first place. He only had himself to blame.

Christmas came, and Fractal was close to despair. He'd had to buy new clothes, but didn't have a washing machine, was forced to use a local laundrette. He no longer shaved properly, was sure that there were uneven patches of stubble on his face... Thought that people at work were looking at him oddly.

On Christmas Eve he tries drinking gin. He's never liked alcohol, but it seems to help. He drinks most of the bottle, goes to the apartment and rings the bell boldly. At first nothing happens – it seems foolish, ringing your own bell. As the door swings inwards, his heart starts to bang. It's Jim, for Christ's sake: pink-shirted, grey-trousered, and blazerless.

'I want to see my wife.' Fractal's voice sounds pointless, as if some mountebank surgeon has implanted a badly performing flute into his chest... Damp trousers cling to his legs, and he remembers he's wearing no coat – only a cheesecloth shirt, and nothing more than espadrilles on his feet. Jim looks pink and at home. His ice-cream hair glows, and he exudes fake goodwill.

'I want to see my children, it's my right.' The note of the defective flute breaks as Fractal is troubled by a sob pushing its way into his mouth. He tries to inch past Jim, but the man's worsted and silk-clad body fills the narrow doorway.

Fractal becomes aware of a weight pressing his espadrilles into the mat well, and as he looks down, he can see that both the man's brown brogues are clamped upon his own flimsy footwear. He's locked to Jim – chin millimetres from the base of the long rubbery neck, and he's aware of the man's breath, bafflingly inoffensive – essence of Love Hearts.

Smiling ever so slightly, the man puckers his lips, and begins to sing:

'When you get in trouble,
and you something, something some,
Give a little wheee whuuu, whee whuuu,
give a little wheee whuuu.'

Fractal can smell the perfumed *wheee whuuu* upon his stinging liquid eyes, and for a moment he closes them in the vain hope that he will wake from the nightmare.

'It's my right,' he implores, the flute within his chest plangent, like a riverboat lost in the fog. His body is being forced backwards as the man leans forwards. Without warning the two plates of brown leather are raised, and Fractal falls onto the stone flags. He shakes his limbs into a squatting position, hears the bang of the front door, and once again he is alone.

Fractal's fingers press wet stone, rub creaking iron. He feels pain in his right knee as he involuntarily genuflects against concrete. His palms scrape gritty brick – can feel sticky fragments of mortar. He tries to hold his face up towards the dark and starless void. The air seems to have turned yellow, and his hair is wet.

He tries to run, first left, then right, on and on… Becomes conscious of a gap between upright railings, wide enough to get his head through, then his shoulders, and the remainder of his filth-caked body. Squatting, he moves forward as if swimming through invisible water… Can feel spiky grass, can smell sap of yew; something stings his lips and cheek. His hands come to rest on vertical stone; fingers can trace incised inscription, and his nose rests against spongy lichen.

He gropes forward, arms resting against stone, through

air, against stone, air; stone, air, stone. There are lines of monoliths, an opening; he leans his shoulder, can hear the groaning of old iron as he squeezes into darkness. It's a retreat with stone walls and sarcophagi where his face no longer feels wet.

Fractal lies on a slab in his cave; for a period of time he can only calculate by seeing dark followed by light, followed by dark... many times. He is not alone. There are other beings in his rock asylum. He can't see or touch them, but he knows they are there.

Sometimes he leaves the security of the chamber and goes to drink from an undulation in a stone-paved path. Once, during the light, he looks up and sees a woman carrying flowers. When she catches sight of him kneeling, naked to the waist, and sucking rainwater, she drops the flowers and runs away. Fractal gathers and places them on the slabs in his chamber. By the time he has returned to sanity and found his way back to the orange brick block on Goldhawk Road, the flowers have died.

'Fract... you okay?' It was Tonal's voice. 'We expected you yesterday – for the completion. It's all signed and sealed, and we got an extra £1.2m because the Lambs Farm contract came good, and that was one of our jobs, not one of Steve Salvo's. He's all set for stock market listing next year. Our financial problems are over!'

Fractal's breath felt hot; the bedsheets – wound round his body – shamefully soiled. 'Whooo, is Steve Salvo?' he exhaled.

'Fract, are you all right? Steve's our new CEO, and

its pronounced Sowvaux, remember?' Of *course*, Fractal had always dealt with other directors, their accountants, solicitors. He'd usually been at Lambs Farm when the head honcho had been in town.

'Tonal, I need to speak to you about something, urgently.'

'Sure. Are you coming in?'

'…With you in an hour.'

Fractal dragged his body out onto the street. It was a miracle he was alive. He had a memory of drinking rainwater, a recollection of swigging gin, and an even more terrible souvenir of the man in the paisley cravat.

But Fractal hadn't just been squatting in an ancient family vault in Brompton Cemetery for nine days in a state of temporary psychosis, drinking rainwater, eating grass. He'd had lucid moments… Been thinking things out. Cassie was right. He'd been an impulsive fool to leave home. He needed to open up to those closest to him; to share, be less secretive. Cassie was a loving mother and partner, his lover and peer. She could be tough, but she was loyal. The situation wasn't irredeemable, and he would start by telling Tonal the whole story. He would see the doctor, talk to a shrink if he had to. Fractal had been to hell and back. He had faced his phantoms of guilt about the house, and his father. He'd squared up to his demons of insecurity, and the worst of them had been Jim.

Jim had been no more than a figment of his imagination… Sure, that blow in the belly had felt real enough, and he was still aware of pain in his toes, but even mental disorders had their physical manifestations – ask someone who's suffered post-traumatic stress! No, he could cope with Jim now, he was sure of that.

'Fraaact, good to see you...' Fractal notices that Tonal is wearing a suit, is gripping his arm, and quivering with excitement. He has the look of a man who's changed – who's *been* changed.

'Come and meet the CEO. Then we'll celebrate, eh?' Tonal's mouth is wide open, both hands raised and vibrating like an architectural Al Jolson.

'Tonal, I need to talk to you.' Fractal follows the heels of Tonal's black Chelsea boots as they bound up the stairs to the conference room. He pads over the limed wood floor, to the cream conference door, and glances through the steel-rimmed porthole. He can see the legs and feet of a man sitting in the white leather, high-backed swivel chair. The man has his back to him, but Fractal has already glimpsed grey-worsted cloth, seen the nutty brown finish of well-polished country brogues.

Tonal's right hand closes round the polished aluminium handle and pulls. He holds open the door.

'Fract, this is Steve Salvo... You meet at last!

Fractal stands stock still as the white leather, high-backed chair creaks and swivels to face him.

THE MAGIC CARPET

'*STOCKHOLM*', that's what the online catalogue said. There's a whole family – a lamp, a table, a sofa, a mirror – nothing to do with the city; it's just a name. Mine is Mohammed – Mo, I prefer – and I work in the City. I'm a global accounts manager, I'm twenty-five, shockingly well paid but don't have much spare time. I don't have a girlfriend either.

IKEA was made for people like me. I click, and it don't matter whether it's *aktad, antilop, backaryd, beboelig, fanigt, fillsta, stig, or sprutt*, it's here in two shakes of a monkey's tail, or two shakes of an *apa's* tail, I guess I should say. Stockholm, by the way, is a rug: 2.4 metres by 1.7.

The day Stockholm arrived, I was crazy busy juggling the Asshole Airlines account with Parmesan Homes, and it was past midnight when I shimmied out of the lift of my apartment block on Upper Thames Street. I could see that the courier had left a parcel outside my door – 1.7 metres long – same height as me, a smidge taller if you allow for the chunky visqueen in which it was wrapped. I dragged it in, dropped it onto the laminate, and glanced at the label before heading for a bit of the old *aqua* treatment. *Hand Woven in India*, it said.

After a good rubba-dub-dub I hit the Egyptian cotton – Heals this time, not IKEA. The old see-slits were firmly shut but those zzzzds were evasive little so-an'-sos… just wouldn't come. It was Pete at Parmesan what was doing it, the manipulative bastard. I'd sussed he was setting a trap for me… Get me off the account so he could have Lo Lo instead of me…

Then I heard it. It was like somebody letting air out of a balloon. At first, I thought it might be the air brakes on some street-cleaning truck, or the coital ceremony coming from the next apartment, but when I went to point Percy at the porcelain, there was no doubt. It was coming from inside that visqueen sheath lying outside my bedroom door.

Shit-'n'-sugar, did I scarper! On went the ear defenders; then it hit me – *Morelia Spilota*. That's what it was. Grandad was always going on about them – said they were lethal… Told me that they'd slither inside the cardboard tube and lie there undetected, sometimes for weeks. 'Carpet buggers', he called them. Gran used to say that a fully grown one was six foot – 1.8 metres in IKEA-speak – but maybe this was a young bastard.

Zzzzds were a no-no now and as I lay rigid – all 1.7 metres of me – perspiring into my zero-allergy pillow (M&S) I thought about the *morelia spilota*… And it wouldn't be in harmless basking mode either; it would be bloody ravenous after being cooped up in cardboard and plastic for god knows how long. They're arboreal – can climb anything. They're particularly partial to crossing things – roads, rivers, rock faces – and they love thresholds. Oh yes, it would relish the journey from laminate to loop pile… and up onto Egyptian cotton… Oh fuck-fuck-fuck! It was all right for *it*, reclining rod-like and displaying its conspicuous set of thermolabile pits to the inner cardboard, but what about me? I was shagged!

Somehow, I slept – I woke up, so I must have done – and by the time I'd pussy-footed back from my dawn pee, and past the polythene tube, I had my plan of action. It was 0400hrs and so instead of waiting until my usual rising hour of 0500, I dressed in Saffredi suit – minus jacket for now – white cotton button-down and dark silk tie. I opened the hall closet, took out a Stanley knife and a new roll of silvery gaffer tape. I tugged open the white-painted sash window in the sitting room, and – taking no chances – pulled on a pair of ribbed motorcycle gauntlets before sliding the packaged carpet across the laminate and heaving it against the windowsill.

Then came the tricky bit and I knew I would have to work like lightning. In one seamless movement I sliced a seventy-five-millimetre hole in the end of the package, thrust the tube *out* of the window and slammed down the sash. Without pausing, I yanked off length after length of gaffer, plastering it across the gap between glass and sill. I stood back and waited.

In a while the *spilota* would come wriggling out in search of food. It would find itself in non-arboreal urban space, coil around the slippery visqueen 'branch', where it would wait to pick off a passing pigeon. If it tried to come back into the apartment, it would get stuck on the gooey barrier I'd built. I could picture its stripy, phallus-like head, gorge gaping and well and truly glued against the gaffer.

I stood, watched, and waited for an hour. Nothing happened – except *something* was happening. It was that sound again, but instead of a noise like the release of high-pressure gas I felt the sensation of human voices… An undulating melody of treble entwining with base. A heavenly descant… It was Palestrina – '*O magnum mysterium et admirable sacramentum ut animalia viderent Dominum nature…*' – and it was coming from inside the rug.

The voice changed: '*Allahu Akbar, Ash-hadu an la ilaha…*' Grandad was never very religious – gave all that stuff up when he came to live in Hanwell. The voice changed again. This time it was *Born in the USA!*

This was heavy-duty craziness. I lunged, tore the gaffer tape from the window frame, and – thump-thump-thumped the parcel back into the room. I grabbed the Stanley, carefully slit the entire length of the parcel, and heaved. Like a warm, soft wave, the rug unfurled, releasing its olfactory comforts of washed wool and crisp mouth-watering jute as it boomed a new resonance: '*…and the glory, the glory of the Lord shall be revealed, and flesh shall see.*' This was the softest, warmest, most tactile MP3 player I could ever imagine. The *spilota* had been a paranoid fantasy of mine, but this was nothing short of a miracle!

For the next few days, I was on autopilot at work. My attention was focussed entirely on Stockholm. *He* – for some reason I'd given the rug a male identity – had a repertoire and quite a range, too. Yes, he could do Nat King Cole, Springsteen, Handel.

I was spending most of my life sprawled within that soft rectangle of 2.4 metres by 1.7. My hand would travel across the velvety tuft pile, would stroke the pert ridges of loop pile.

I would even adopt a *sajdah* – not for religious reasons, but because I was sure that I could smell Teen Spirit. How low!

When I say *repertoire*, what I mean is that when all this started, I'd assumed that *he* would have a stock of choral works which he would circulate, like a tape on loop, but the list seemed endless. Some pieces I recognised, others I'd never heard before... But something very odd was happening. It was as if Stockholm and I were developing a personal relationship, as if we were exchanging telepathic messages. I would think of a piece and he would perform it – giving it his one hundred per cent wool rendition.

Because I'd been so busy listening to Stockholm, I realised that I hadn't really *looked* at the rug – I mean its pattern, its colours. At first it appeared to be the vaguely stripy design I'd chosen from the internet catalogue, but as time went by, I noticed that it seemed different. There was a hidden landscape – rocks, trees, flowers – but undefined as if coloured inks had been spilled and were running into one another. The tufted surfaces looked dabbed, melted; images seemed scalloped and appeared to be fret-cut. Sometimes the loop pile glowed as if it were made from obsidian.

There were traces of figures; men wearing baggy trousers and headdresses like swollen onions. I began to think that I was in there – one of those curly-moccasined, moustachioed, hookah-smoking dudes – and I didn't like it. Stockholm – it seemed to me – was indulging in just a teeny-weeny bit of racial stereotyping. I rolled him up to the muffled accompaniment of *Pack up your Troubles* and went back to concentrate on Asshole Airlines and Parmesan Homes. I was just in time; Lo Lo had been to the CEO and to get back on track I had to do a few all-nighters.

My boss maybe recognised the signs of strain and suggested that instead of working a third all-nighter I go to a drinks party. One of our clients was fundraising for Macmillan Nurses, so not *entirely* a night off… They were all oldsters – nobody under thirty-five.

'You couldn't meet a lovelier guy, Mo,' enthused host Jim as he introduced me to stocky brachycephalic Colin. Threadbare beard, honest eyes, and a schoolteacher, would you believe? I've never been great at secrets – even though I've had to keep schtum about lots of things because of my job. But something got hold of me and within two texts of an IKEA courier I'd told Colin about the rug. I didn't for a moment think he'd believe me; I just thought it would make a great story. It must be something to do with being a schoolteacher… Must be amazing to actually *believe* in people.

'You should make money out of it!'

I could not believe what the teacher was telling me. Why is it that people who know nothing about making money are always eager to tell you that you should make it? I mean… my annual bonus is ten times what he makes in a year. Don't get me wrong, I don't *mean* to make money; I can't help it. I'm competitive; I have a need to do good shit, and if that means screwing the guy next to me, that's what I'll do.

After the drinks do, he gave me a lift back in his little *skoda*. Why should *I* drive to work when the company provides free cabs?

'Is it just you here, no partner?' Colin seemed curious.

I showed him the rug… He didn't go *wow* or anything, just smiled, and seemed to take it all in his stride. Then he asked if he could be my agent!

'All right…'

Stockholm had spent the last couple of days rolled up under the glass table and I'd been glad to get away from him. There was a threadbare directness about Colin which I liked, and he seemed to like me – said he'd introduce me to his daughter.

'…Same age as you… Work, work, work, that's all she ever talks about… She's an accounts manager with J Walter Thoreson, the advertising agents.'

At first, I left Colin to it. I was glad to be shot of Stockholm. I ordered another rug – John Lewis this time – got the courier to unpack, unroll, and signed for it, but only after I was one hundred per cent sure that it was a silent one.

After that I didn't see much of Colin, but I heard about him, didn't I? …From Melissa. Ye-es we went on a couple of dates, nice girl. She said Colin was 'doing kids' parties'. That way, people didn't ask questions… Parents thought it was a conjuring trick, while Colin was charging them a fortune – fortune to *him*, that is. You see, the thing about us Generation 'Y'ers is we *understand* the value of money. We appreciate that it's no good waiting until things happen to you; *you* have to *make* them happen. Then I met Fluff.

Now, you're thinking namby-pamby-airy-fairy '*floppy-tied aesthetical craftsman*' type, but he *the shit* scared out of me. He was waiting outside the door in Upper Thames and the bastard manhandled me.

'Fluff!'

I wasn't sure whether he was introducing himself or if it was a term of abuse. '*You…* have got something.'

It was that understated patois and I knew *exactly* what

EMPIRE
STATE

A HISTORY

he was on about. He'd got me up against the acid-etched doors – all 1.95 metres of him. Kindling thin, dark kit but grubby, he looked like a degenerate poet from the streets of nineteenth-century Montparnasse. Jet birds-nest *barnet* pricking my ear, carbon Cubans pressing down on my loafers. He was the first person I'd seen who looked more sinister *without* shades than with, and as he whipped them clear of his face, I felt the worst abdominal cramp ever.

'What?'

'*You* know!'

He had me by the Saffredi lapels and I could feel the increased pressure from his Cubans.

'So?' I attempted truculence.

'He works for *me*, and he works for *free*!'

What was this, art for art's sake?

'*You* have been warned.' With that, he stamped the hell out of my left loafer, shoved me hard against the acid-etched, and vanished.

'Fuck-fuck-fuck.' Was that really me squealing?

'Colin... er... it's Mo... How's it going?
'*Fiiine, when are you coming to a show, Mo?*

It's one of those roomy Chelsea studio houses near Flood Street; lots of oak – oldy arts and crafts-style and tall windows which seem to rise up and just keep on going. As I pull on the olde-iron bell, I have an odd feeling, as if I'm being watched. Not by Tatiana, who opens the door, but by something a little more distant. *She* – Tatiana – doesn't introduce herself, but I know that's what she's called because I can hear Brad's voice coming from somewhere on high.

'Tatiana, answer the goddamned door, will ya!'

'Brad and Nisi,' Colin had said, 'oh, and *Ash*ley.' Yes, he'd said it *just* like that.

I follow Tatiana's vermillion *derriere* across the ringing white *carrara* and up the wide oaky stairway. No need for a guide; it's obvious where I'm headed. The sound from above is… almost indescribable. The best I can do is to say that it's like somebody's trying to force Stockholm down a waste-disposal unit.

As I pass through the baronial double doors leading off the landing, I glance to my left – out the window. There it is, looking up: a figure, lanky, kindling-thin, funereal black jacket four sizes too small, drainpipe trousers and hair like a crows' nest. I can sense a general feeling of ill, intangible but like gamma rays, invisible, dangerous, and travelling straight for me.

Tatiana vanishes, and for a split second I shut my mind off from the din. The room I'm standing in is like a medieval hall, and one that's been cleared of furniture. There's a minstrel's gallery – carved, fret-cut, scalloped – and something is already feeling curiously familiar to me. There are twenty small children, fifteen adults – half of whom are female – sitting lotus position, kneeling on brightly coloured yoga mats or leaning against darkly patterned cushions, and all eager-looking. Some of the adults are flitting from group to group where *eat the jelly*, *food on a string*, and *what's on the tray* are in progress.

Most of the children are dressed simply in coloured tops and pants. There's an African girl with bright green shirt and yellow trousers, a carroty-coloured toddler in blue – her carroty mother leaning over her shoulder… A tiny boy wearing over-sized spectacles and a twizzly bow tie, like Brains.

Standing in the middle of the room is a girl, larger than the other children... Puffed-up pink frock, pink roses perched on pyrite hair...

'...Our gorgeous li'l princess!'

My hand is encased in a grip, powerful enough to be threatening. A charcoal cut-away tee stretches dangerously over the man's upper body, while black raw denim jeans are rammed into hunting boots, which look as if they were made from poured pitch. '...Brad!' bellows the man. 'Er... Nisi's not so well – having a lie down.' Colin *had* said something about a 'lush problem with Nisi'.

Then I catch sight of *them*.

At the end of the hall and visible in sudden spokes of sunlight... there's this enormous great catafalque, carved in ebony-hued wood, upon which sits Stockholm... And it's not the homey stripy *catalogue* Stockholm; it's the stained and inky Stockholm; the dabbed and melted images, the arabesques and curlicues, and those onion-headed figures hovering above its quicksilver surface... And there, right at the centre of its 2.4 metres by 1.7, sitting cross-legged, dressed in an Utsav silk tunic with Nerhu collar, moccasined, false-moustachioed and hands in *anjali mudra*, is Colin.

'We're going to play Grandmother's Footsteps, children,' announces Carroty Mum. Stockholm opens up with a hungry 'A Hunting We Will Go'. Li'l Princess is 'Grandmother'. The other children tiptoe towards her turned back, as she stands with hands outstretched, *pinkies* extended. Brad's lower jaw is thrusting... But there's a problem; Princess don't swing fast enough because her pyrite curls are shedding pink flowers and before you can shout 'Ginny Doll', Brains and the yellow-trousered African girl are upon her.

It's a similar story with Musical Statues, and all those exciting hats and coloured cloaks which have been waiting to be donned in Dressing Up Dancing just won't fit Princess without a major wardrobe adjustment.

'Where the hell's Tatiana?' Brad's poured leg wear and feet are stomping the parquet. The other children are well into Musical Bumps to the accompaniment of Hickory Dickory Dock, and I'm getting a strange feeling that some of them are sitting down rather more firmly than they want to as I hear yelps of pain. One of the dads seems to have developed a nervous tic, and several of the adults are behaving as if they're being bitten by fleas.

'Can we have something a little calmer?' Carroty Mum leads a sing-song as Stockholm unravels a decidedly fleecy 'Frère Jacques'… And all this time Colin hasn't spoken – hasn't moved – he's gone transcendental!

'How Much is That Doggie in the Window' sounds fine until the doggie barks and it's a howl like *An American Werewolf in London*. Some of the children are in tears. Carroty Mum tiptoes backwards and forwards, hands alternating between being in homily and touching tiny heads. 'Do Re Mi', she demands, but after the first few bars it turns into the choral works of Stockhausen. Carroty tries to get the children to play Sleepy Lions, but nobody will lie down and arguments have broken out among the adults.

Tippy tippy tap toe on your shoulder, I shall be your master – no, that's not right, it's *you shall be my partner*. Everything's going wrong and it's not me, honest! Instead of tapping, the children are really socking one another. Brains' spectacles go flying off as he gets a punch from a fat boy. Princess screams, sits down hard on the parquet, and five kids pile on top of her. I can hear a voice in my head: '*He works for me and he works for free.*'

'You bastard…!' Out of the corner of my right eye I can see Brad's right finger wagging in my direction. It's time for Colin and me to make our escape. Please don't let him be in a coma!

Somehow, I rouse Colin; we rock and tug Stockholm into a roll, and run like hell for the double doors.

'I'll sue every bone in your goddamned body!' For a moment I think that Brad is upon us, but there's a new sound coming from inside Stockholm. As we helter-skelter down the oaky, I hear the elephantine crash of brass, and the eerie tenor of Benjamin Britten's 'Lyke Wake Dirge'. I hear screams coming from upstairs – and they're not all children. As we wrench open the front door and tumble over the threshold, there's the mournful sound of a siren.

'Oh, Jesus, someone's called an ambulance.'

Well, all that was forty years ago! …And I'm *still* married to that young lady that Colin introduced me to. Oh, yes, we got through the kids' party stage years ago, we're grandparents now – real oldsters.

Colin was the loveliest father-in-law you could *ever* wish for. He passed on to be with the great events manager in the sky five years ago, bless his little sateen tunic. *Events*, that's what we did. I quit the City, Melissa packed in the 'hidden persuader' industry, and we formed a family business… All

kosher, no bloody magic carpets, I can tell you! We went on courses and that – Melissa insisted!

But I know what you're *thinking*…

Stockholm? Tate Modern wouldn't have him 'very dodgy provenance'. MoMA said, 'No,' and Saatchi? – not a chance. Eventually we got him into a *lovely* little gallery in Norwich – on compassionate grounds. I've got the covenant here 'cos I knew you'd be asking…

'…*the said art gallery to be free of charge at all times to members of the public, and in the case of the establishment changing ownership and new management requiring entry fees, then an alternative, non-fee-charging establishment be found…*'

They do go on a bit, these solicitors.

'…And Fluff…?'

'Fluff to you, mate!'

THE ART OF
OWNERSHIP

Hereward struts into the dining room and gazes gloomily out to sea. The mist of the early morning has cleared and it's a *glorious* day. Trees are glowing like nuggets of gold, and the water on the estuary shining like a giant plate of silver.

From a distant part of his estate, he can hear the drumming of a woodpecker, and just outside the window, a dove breaks free of its perch in an alder and a thousand fat little catkins swing backwards and forwards, releasing a tower of pollen into the warming air.

It's so unlike how Hereward feels inside. There's something hanging over him… A dark cloud… A collection of gases; grubby, menacing, and coalescing inside his head. He's got to face facts – but please, not yet; later…

His eye comes to rest on the baize-like surface of the lawn outside the window, and he recalls the night twenty years ago when he danced. Not upon this lawn, but on the modest square of grass which had been the garden of his semi-detached in… somewhere no longer important. It had been the night his mother died, and he became certain that he would inherit a fortune large enough to purchase Penn'th Hall.

The telephone call had come in the early morning. He'd gone outside, and in the glow from the sodium light, had slowly and deliberately performed a stately dance while muttering the words of J B Morton's 'Dancing Cabman' which he had learned at school. A poem about a cabman who dances alone on a lawn wearing his bowler hat in celebration of his dead aunt who has just left him a fortune.

Hereward could contain himself no longer, and as he stretched out his arms and kicked with his feet, he shouted his own peculiar version of the final line:

'And his mother is dead!'

Then he held his knuckles against his teeth. He did not want to wake his wife, Sweetsmile, who was asleep in the front bedroom.

'Fifty-five acres of woodland, Grade 2 listed. A stunning elevated setting over the estuary…' the estate agent's details had said. *'…A well-stocked garden and a viewing platform from which Lord Nelson and Lady Hamilton had once looked out…'*

Hereward can feel a sob forcing its way into his mouth. He turns, takes two paces, and, with almost superhuman force, brings his hand down – smack – on the huge, polished mahogany table. He's conscious of a sound, senses a rush of air, and like a house owner who has just surprised a burglar in the dead of night, he expels the sob, in one great howl.

'Fuckingbastard…!'

The nights had been long. He and Sweetsmile had separate

47

rooms; she didn't seem to mind – just kept smiling sweetly. He'd spent a lot of time hunched over his computer. At first it was *Casino*, after that – *Double Vegas*; then *3D Roulette* seemed more attractive. There were unofficial websites where stakes were higher, excitement more intense.

He dared not tell Sweetsmile what he had done. He had never known a time when she had not smiled.

A hundred miles away, Aria sat in his office, peering into the perfect surface of his glass table. It was like a pool of infinite depth, and he was convinced that if he asked it a question, it would give an answer.

The rejoinder came in the form of a shout from his assistant Eljah, who was making coffee in the office kitchen.

'You're number fifty-five in the rich list, Aria. That's up ten from last year!'

Aria wasn't his real name; his wife always called him that because of his love of music. They adored Mozart and Beethoven, and even before their seven children were born, she had called him Aria. Sometimes it would be 'Aria Cantabile'; on other occasions she would refer to him as 'Aria Agitata', and even 'Aria di Bravura'! The two of them knew many pieces by heart, and would – when the mood took them – strike up a duet. It really was most charming.

Eljah noiselessly set down the coffee cup in front of Aria. Everything Eljah did was careful, thoughtful, and Aria knew that Eljah liked working for him because Aria was a man of great fairness and – in spite of his wealth – a man of modesty. He was tall – six foot four and a quarter – with a powerful chest, but his wife always told him that he was as soft as a lamb. He really was a very nice man.

He studied his reflection in the oval mirror which he had hung on the wall opposite his desk. With his long dark beard and pince-nez spectacles, he smiled at the thought that he bore more than a passing resemblance to a character in an illustration by Edmund Dulac. He loved all those stories: *The Princess and the Pea, Ali Baba and the Forty Thieves, Treasure Island*... He adored everything which was British... Knew by heart all the kings and queens of England that there had ever been.

Aria's grandparents had been refugees from a European city. He'd done well... Been blessed with many children, owned numerous properties, and had a lovely house. But that wasn't enough for Aria. He wanted to give back to those from whom he had benefitted. He supported charities, gave money; yet there was still something missing.

Things hadn't all been easy. The northern city in which he lived sometimes erupted in violence. There had been hatred. What Aria most wanted, was to feel that he belonged, to have a home that he really owned; really owned.

Hereward and Sweetsmile had no children. Since they had purchased Penn'th Hall, the two of them lived on the uppermost of its three floors. Guests came – though no more than one at a time, so when Stiv did her daily rounds of the eighteen rooms – not counting bathroom and toilets – she was cleaning rooms which had been unoccupied, often for months.

When the evenings were long and the weather mild, Hereward and Sweetsmile would walk in the grounds, admiring the work of their gardener Div. Better still, they would venture deep into the woodland of the estate, sometimes play hide and seek. He searched; she *always* hid. She really was so very coy.

When it rained, they would walk round the rooms of the house… Across the hall, round the drawing room, and through the library. They would gently perambulate the circular sunroom, take a tour of the study, stroll through the bedrooms, and arrive back at the dining room, where they would climb up onto the deep windowsill and stand, staring out into the fastness beyond the glass. Hereward thought that Sweetsmile looked like a gentle little doll. She was five feet tall; he was no more than five feet four.

People said they'd been just right for one another… Met at art college in the 1960s… Spent hours walking up and down Kings Road and going to 'gigs'. They were the 'perfect couple', always found the best flats to rent with the least furniture in them – which they always painted white. They discovered the most exquisite clothes in the second-hand markets, and Sweetsmile could make herself look just like Arthur Rackham's illustrations of Peter Pan's Wendy.

The wedding almost hadn't happened. Her family had paid for the semi-detached, and although Sweetsmile smiled throughout the register office ceremony, Hereward thought that her old man looked as if he had little to smile about. Hereward's money had come much later.

His dad had been a taxi driver from Plaistow, died from a coronary, leaving Mum little else to live on other than the state pension… But there *had* been something else: *patents*, for mining lamps designed by Grandad, who'd been an inventor. Years back, the designs had been sold to international mining companies in exchange for big blocks of shares. As the shares soared and dividends poured in,

Mum just carried on, living the frugal life she had always known. Remember that day she forgot to lock the drawer where she kept her bank statements? 'Jesus! There *was* bloody millions,' and Hereward was the sole heir!

He felt sick again, but the cloud which had been hanging over him was beginning to clear. He could feel a plan forming in his mind. But not yet; he was still not ready. He would wait a little longer...

Sweetsmile would only leave the house to visit her dressmaker and the two of them would eat lunch together in the town. Hereward liked nothing better than a 'takeaway' eaten straight out of its foil container. He would drive to the shop in his Lamborghini, park it on the pavement, and enjoy watching the lustful expressions of those waiting in line for saveloy and chips. It was so fucking down to earth. It also meant time off for their cook, Liv.

Hereward liked rock music... No time for classical, not enough oomph. So, when Sweetsmile drove one of their five automobiles into the town, he would stay in and 'give it some welly'.

When he had filled the deserted house and grounds with sound, he would parade up and down the wide corridors, strutting along and punching the air. He was partial to stamping with both feet, right hand raised to his chin, elbow stuck out in front, left fist behind him as if he was doing the crawl. At the sound of a particularly muscular 'riff', he would leap into the air.

Once, he had landed badly, hurt his back, but his mobile telephone still lay within reach and he was able to call

Div, Liv, and Stiv – it took all three – to carry him to his narrow bed where he lay in pain for some time. He had told Sweetsmile that it had been a bad headache.

Hereward was feeling better. Now was the moment; he would telephone Womble the estate agent and explain his plan. He left the 'top-end' guitar solo playing on the hi-fi while he spoke to his friend.

Although they had spoken on the telephone, Womble insisted on having what he referred to as a 'hair-to-hair'. In Hereward's case, this would have to be a 'hair-to-bald head'. There was no shortage of photographs throughout the hall showing the hirsute Hereward, but they had been taken many years ago, and as time passed, all he had been left with was a very shiny, round, red head.

Little estate agency business took place in the town below Penn'th Hall. Few people wanted to live there. Some folk did arrive by accident, though almost invariably Womble's office was deserted, which was why it had become a meeting place for Hereward and his friends.

These friends all embraced the Rock Culture – or 'Rock Media', as Hereward preferred to call it.

'We are the Stone Circle!' Womble would chuckle darkly. Hereward saw the group as a kind of Masonic union – without all that trouser-rolling mumbo-jumbo. There was a long-haired barrister from the next town, a leather clerk of the court, a studded and bejewelled retired planning officer, and even a rock judge known as Nudge.

Nudge – it transpired, as Hereward arrived at Womble's office and gripped the man's steel-bangled and tattooed forearm – was due to appear in court in a week's time. Not behind the bench, but in front of it. The long-haired justice had decked someone outside a takeaway shop. Womble brandished a copy of *The Blodwyn Bugle*, displaying the headline 'Rock Judge in Kebab Row'.

Hereward squatted across a chair, arms draped over its moth-eaten upholstery as he outlined his scheme, while Womble produced from a drawer a peculiarly bloated roll-up cigarette, which he waved backwards and forwards before snapping down on it with his lighter.

'I don't want any Tom, Dick, or Harry, turning up to view the house when it goes on the market,' insisted Hereward. 'I need to keep as much control over the property, after the sale, as it's possible to do…' Womble blinked. His hand wandered behind his head where it began to fidget with his pigtail. He fixed Hereward with a stare, eyes like pools of black oil.

'Control…' Womble repeated, sounding as if he was in the grip of a heavy head cold. '…Control, is what we all want in this world…' His eyes closed. 'The thing is…' he intoned, nose plugged with invisible wadding, words punctuated with painful intakes of breath, '…the thing is… it's the wrong people who have got at the controls.'

'What I mean is…' Hereward felt his voice rising an octave, '…is there any way I can obtain a deed of covenant, so I can force the buyer to use my contractors and architects, on any work they might do later?'

The entire office was a cloud of smoke, and Womble had acquired the appearance of a Russian Orthodox priest about to incant liturgical mass. 'He do big squeal like holy Trichpatte.'

'Cov-en-nant,' he breathed, his Episcopalian-like body leaning forward, hairy stalactite of a beard almost touching Hereward's red nose. He looked grave.

'That, sounds like a toke… a toke on a veeery powerful spliff.'

Womble leaned back creakily in his chair as he exhaled with world-ending ferocity… Raised his right hand – as if to beatify: 'Worry not, my friend, fortune will fall right into your lap when you least expect it.'

Aria had been following a trail of blood on the pavement near his office. He couldn't decide which end was the starting point, and where the finish might be. Nor could he piece together events which might have caused such blood-letting. It would be nothing more sinister than a nosebleed, he reasoned.

Back at his desk he found himself fondly recollecting holidays he spent as a child, by the Welsh or English seaside.

'Here's something that might suit you, Aria.' It sounded promising; it was one of the seaside locations he remembered. There were mountains, waterfalls, heather-covered moors, castles – no, it was more than promising – it looked ideal. *All applications and telephone conversations treated in strict confidence*, it said.

Eljah keyed in the number and handed the set to Aria.

'Hello, my name is Aria. I'd like more information about Penn'th Hall.' There was a silence at the other end of the phone, followed by a dark chuckle.

'I'm glad you're not called Tom or Dick!' Aria quite liked the joke. The voice sounded like a cockney one. He didn't think he'd ever met a cockney, but he had heard that they were 'the salt of the earth'.

As he put the phone down, Aria felt punch-drunk. He was reeling from the interrogation he'd received. Was he prepared to submit to a credit check? How long would he be planning to stay in the house? Would he be selling it on in a few years? Would he be having guests there? What changes did he plan to make?

It appeared that the vendor would be retaining ten of the fifty-five acres and was in the process of obtaining planning permission to build a bungalow for himself and his wife on the site. It would be nice to have a close neighbour.

'*Porgi, amor, qualche ristoro…*' Mrs Aria was in full spate as the people carrier containing herself and Aria, the seven children, two aunts, an uncle, his mother – and, of course, Eljha – sped along the motorway.

'*Voi chespete che cosa e amoi…*' she continued. Aria would respond when the appropriate moment came. Occasionally they would steal one another's parts and burst into laughter. Some of the older children knew odd fragments of word and melody. *The Marriage of Figaro* was a real family favourite, and Mrs Aria would sometimes joke that they would become like the Von Trapp family in *The Sound of Music*. When a reference to a certain location occurred in the libretto, Mrs Aria substituted Penn'th Hall. *It was so funny*, thought Aria, *so witty*. They would soon be arriving for the viewing.

Long before he heard the sound of rubber on gravel, Hereward had seen the sun winking on the windscreen of

the black people carrier as it made its way through the forest drive. It almost seemed as if somebody was signalling to him. He hoped that it was a good sign.

Hurrying from the huge 'L'-shaped lounge, he scuttled along the corridor, across the inner hall, and took up position in the outer hall. Sweetsmile was already there, and dressed completely in white. Standing in the centre of the space, so small under the tall Ionic columns, she looked like an Alice who had recently swallowed the contents of the 'drink me' bottle. Hereward was wearing his usual Levi 501s, but nicely finished off with a welcoming scarlet, skin-tight shirt, unbuttoned almost to the waist.

The vehicle flashed past the window. Hereward wrenched open the double doors and marched across the forecourt. As the people carrier came to a halt, every one of its doors sprang open simultaneously, and what appeared to Hereward to be a troupe of circus performers, dressed entirely in black and white, tumbled onto the gravel.

As he and Aria shook hands, Hereward became acutely aware of the fact that the topmost button of his own red shirt was approximately level with where the tall man's penis would be – buried deep somewhere in those black trousers. How he wished Womble had agreed to conduct the viewing on his behalf.

Hereward felt uncomfortable amongst the mass of smiling aunts, uncles, and bouncing children. For a moment it reminded him of the Lord Nelson Coach Trips, which Heritage had organised before he and Sweetsmile could stand it no longer and brought them to an end.

Some of the children had already swept past him, were inside the hall, and as he was propelled backwards by the giant black-bearded pince-nezed figure, he felt a feeling of dread. It wasn't meeting people who belonged to an ethnic minority which troubled him – he and Sweetsmile had known people at art college who were black. They'd thought that had been 'very cool'; but all these children? Who, in this day and age…?

At first when Hereward re-entered the hall, he thought that Sweetsmile had vanished altogether. Then he caught sight of her, withdrawn to the far side of the room and perched on the topmost tread of a small flight of portable library steps, as if she was escaping from a mouse. Standing there, she looked like a tiny porcelain figurine on its own base, smiling – eyes glistening with a special glaze.

The youngest children had disappeared from sight, and the two aunts set off in different directions to try and find them. An appealing little girl with dark ringlets emerged from her hiding place. Hereward was amused to see that she was dragging behind her a green wellington boot; he was a great believer in free expression. But when a tiny boy entered from another direction with Hereward's flying jacket draped round his shoulders, he felt sudden panic. Upstairs were unlocked cupboards of his – which even Sweetsmile and Stiv would never dream of entering. There were personal items concealed there, which if paraded like this could cause embarrassment beyond belief. Hereward felt a crimson flush, accompanied by a fearful perspiration.

The highlight of the viewing turned out to be the swimming pool. Not that it existed yet, but Hereward had obtained planning permission, and an animated discussion arose as to what depth it might be, how warm the water could

be, and so on. Sweetsmile had long since retired for a 'lie down'.

Hereward contemplated his plan. There were no orthodox schools in the vicinity; no places of worship. Aria and his family would only be here on holidays, and then for short periods. Though he loathed with all his heart the idea of living in the bungalow, playing custodian to the hall and its new owner, it could be to his benefit. Things would not be easy for Aria. He recollected Womble's chuckle and what he referred to as the 'philosophy' of the Stone Circle. 'We,' mouthed Womble, his stalactite of a beard wagging to and fro, 'are like the robin, the thrush, and the blackbird, *we* do not migrate.'

Contracts for sale had been exchanged. Aria had been taken aback by the news that there had been no other bids. Eljah had encouraged him to negotiate for a lower price but Aria had said, 'If that is the asking price, then so be it; it's worth so much more to me.' It had been love at first sight, and now, standing again in the outer lobby at Penn'th, he loved it more than ever.

This time he had left his family at home, apart from Mrs Aria – and Eljah, of course. Aria had gathered his architect and interior designer, was briefing them on the changes he was going to make. Money no object; he and his team would do everything, just as heritage required. He would be the owner – but Penn'th Hall was part of national heritage, and for him it would be a kind of stewardship.

Mr and Mrs Hereward looked different from when he had last seen them. She was dressed in a pale grey linen suit, while Mr Hereward had donned a navy shirt with a Mandarin collar which he wore outside his trousers. Aria experienced an inexplicable feeling of unease.

The briefing tour of the house took all day. Mr Hereward repeatedly insisted that he would 'go off and leave them all to it', but only once did he depart Aria's side – to visit the bathroom. Mrs Hereward engaged the architect in fervent conversation, and they seemed to be getting along like a house on fire. Aria would have liked to have talked with his own team more, but it was important that they bonded with the Herewards. They really were such a very attentive couple.

Mr Hereward had thought of everything. He had organised his surveyor to draw up plans of the house, arranged for an engineer to call; had even obtained books on interior design styles which he set down on the huge mahogany dining table with such a flourish. When the tour was over, and the team gone, Mr Hereward took Aria's arm and led him into the study. Hereward's face had the look of a teacher whose student has just made a howling error.

'I'm concerned...' he frowned, 'that these consultants aren't up to the job.' Aria's heart sank. They were his team, he believed in them, they trusted one another, had worked together – known one another for years.

'*He* didn't have the experience. *She* had too far to travel.' Aria was struck by how shrill Mr Hereward's voice sounded. '*He* might upset the local planning officers. *She* didn't know enough about materials.' It was a blow, but Mr Hereward was right; after all, who knew Penn'th Hall and its surroundings better than he? Mr Hereward even had good local legal friends. They were down-to-earth men, the backbone of Britain.

'You know, Aria, you should stand up to him more, it's going to be your house, not his.' Eljah's hands rested carefully on the wheel of the black Mercedes limousine as it sped north.

'I think it will be a symbiotic relationship.' Aria was staring straight ahead. '…Symbiotic, my foot!' Eljah snapped his fingers. '…Biological jargon hijacked by sociologists. It describes low-life forms – like fungus and algae oxygenating one other to produce lichen, parasites 'grooming' larger animals, little fish living off big ones… Nothing to do with human relationships; human beings are far more complex!'

Eljah could be outspoken, and Aria valued what he had to say. He wasn't going to fall out with him now, but his mind was made up.

Aria gazed out of the dining-room window. He was watching a pheasant tiptoeing across the lawn. With its scarlet head, shot-green yolk, and shiny black underbelly, it looked magnificent as it ruffled its feathers, gave its ratchetty screech and took off over the trees, which grew right down to the water's edge. Through the open window, Aria could hear the excited shouts of the children as they splashed around in the swimming pool.

The building work had been completed in record time. Mr Hereward's team really had 'known their stuff' – as Hereward had put it. There were a few things which Aria hadn't been happy about, but they were small things, trifles; the point was, everything was complete, everybody was settled. The Herewards were comfortably moved into their bungalow. They really were *so* attentive.

Whenever Aria and his family arrived at the hall, Mr and Mrs Hereward would always be there – standing by the open front door. Once, Aria found them both at attention, on either side of the door like two tiny sentries.

Everything inside the house would always be ready and perfect. Div, Liv, and Stiv were still there. Mrs Aria had been upset about that – she had her own people – but Aria had soon talked her round. Who knew Penn'th Hall better than they?

Hereward strutted into the dining room of his bungalow and gazed out to sea. He had made a mistake about that swimming pool. The light on the water in the estuary shone like a giant plate of silver, but the surface of the pool looked like some foreign blue cocktail quivering in its glass. It really was quite out of place.

Two summers had passed since the time he had looked out in his misery and formed his little plan. Things hadn't turned out so badly after all. Aria's children were growing up; the oldest boys now often went out into the town – in the summer evenings when the days were long.

Hereward's mobile hummed in the pocket of his Levis. It was Aria, something was wrong, and Hereward could hear a horrible panting noise at the other end of the phone… Aria and Mrs Aria had just returned from the hospital several miles away… An incident the evening before… Two of the boys attacked in the town… Schlomo dead as a result of his injuries.

'…Dreadful! Appalling! A tragedy…' Hereward heard his own voice, yet he felt a strange sensation of excitement. It was as if he had ingested some drug which made his mouth tingle, tickled his stomach. Neither he nor Sweetsmile went to the funeral; it would have meant travelling.

It's three in the morning, and Hereward cannot sleep. His old urge has returned. The laptop lies only feet away from his narrow bed and he can feel that collection of gases: grubby, menacing, and coalescing inside his head. When his mobile hums, he nearly jumps out of his skin.

It's Aria; he sounds apologetic.

'No, no, no, not at all… I was awake.' Hereward can feel his mouth tingling again, stomach tickling. Months have passed since the tragedy, and he has seen nothing of Aria. It seems that the man has no plan for visiting the hall for 'the foreseeable future'.

'Of course, selling is out of the question. It will always be one of the great loves of my life. What happened wasn't the fault of the hall!' Hereward can feel himself breathing hard.

'In view of this, would you and Mrs Hereward like to move back into the top floor?' Hereward can feel anticipation uncoiling within him.

'It could be a bit like old times.' There's a wistful little laugh at the other end of the phone. 'You've been such perfect neighbours.'

The excitement in Hereward's body suddenly seems to surge, as if something beyond his control has released a charge of electricity. His limbs taut like some artificially created creature, he struts out of the bungalow and swaggers up to the hall.

The tall windows look cold and white, as they reflect a giant full moon which hangs in the sky, while ten million stars blaze in worshipful silence.

Hereward stands in the centre of the green baize lawn and, slowly and deliberately, he performs a stately dance while murmuring the words of that poem. He can contain

himself no longer, and as he reaches the final line, he shouts out over the estuary his own peculiar version:

'And his son is dead!'

Hereward holds his knuckles against his teeth. He must not wake Sweetsmile, who is asleep in the front bedroom of the bungalow.

As Hereward stretches out his arms, it seems as if he is holding the full moon in his hand. *He* alone is the rightful master of Penn'th Hall, and at the end of each of his outstretched fingers is a tiny, burning star.

FALSE MIRROR

'm watching you!

What I mean is, I'm watching *him*. A man. He's wearing a flattened straw hat, cheesecloth shirt and grubby white chinos. Can't see what he's got on his feet. He's hesitating, grasping ropes on either side of him. Ropes are as thick as your fist. He leans forward, puts his right foot in front of his left, and begins to walk.

Amazing, how much a rope bridge moves when it's got someone on it. The quivering is unbelievable! You'd think that with all that miles of rope, millions of strands that go into making it, that it would be rigid, but it's not. It's as if the man is trying to walk on jelly. I can't hear his breathing from where I'm standing, but his heart must be going like the clappers. All that movement, and everything around him so still! There's no wind, no birdsong, no rustling of leaves, and even the river is so far below that you can't hear anything.

The man reaches the middle of the bridge. I can't believe the amount of sag on the ropes. He can't be that heavy. The climb to the other side will be so steep, I doubt if he'll have the strength to make it – and there's another problem. There's a hole in the floor of the bridge. The man reaches into the right pocket of his chinos and pulls out a ball of string. I feel like laughing. Repairing it with that little ball of fuzz? It's like expecting to cut a hedge with nail scissors. But he's doing it, and gingerly he crosses – balancing on the cat's cradle he's created. It might well take *his* weight, but I'm doubtful it would take mine, and it's only now that I realise that there is considerable urgency for me to follow this guy. There's a cluster of people coming down the mountain path who will have to use the bridge also.

I step onto the bridge; it shudders under me, and I'm straining every sinew to try and make myself as light as possible. I glance behind me and see that there's quite a procession about to step onto the ropes. Having watched the man in front of me struggle to complete this apparently Herculean task, I'm surprised at the ease with which I haul myself up. I'm not carrying a smartphone, so once across, I find a telephone box and call the police – anonymously. I feel certain that someone following me is bound to fall to their death, but I'm not prepared to disclose my name. Secrecy is essential on all fronts, and I must never do anything which might alert the attention of the man I am following.

'Enjoy your dreams!' psychologists say. 'The unconscious has its own elegant logic. The flow of mystery is intense.' But being asleep is not the same as being unconscious, and, like Alice, we can all enjoy a certain sense of control. 'It's only a dream!' When *I* fall down the rabbit hole, I've developed a special type of smugness, even smugger than Alice's indignance – if that's possible. I make a point of taking risks. I court mischief, and if I find myself in an erotically compromising position, then believe me, I go for it! There will be no consequences to endure when one awakes.

It's the same man, and this time he's swimming – which means that I am, too, because I'm following him. Concealment is a prerequisite. It's night time, and we're in a moonlit river, or it could be a canal – but whichever it is, it's dirty. There's flotsam, including a murky scum whose froth I have to part with my breast stroking hands. My kicking legs hit submerged objects, some of which resist with the inertia of metallic objects. Other foreign bodies yield, shift, and float away to different locations. The depth of liquid in which I'm floating seems variable, and as I swim, I notice the occasional partly submerged supermarket trolley. On either side of the watercourse, there are buildings redolent of abandoned factories, decaying freighters, and industrial ruins.

The man grasps at a set of steel steps fixed to the edge of the canal and hauls himself out of the water. I follow, keeping at a safe distance. He enters the vast, shadowy volume of a factory building. It's a sinister cathedral of decay and grime into which I'm compelled to pursue, picking my way under steel gantries, past lowering jibs, and squeezing between brown, flaking, steel pylons. I cross bridges whose welded steel plates are full of jagged holes, and I notice that what were once metal handrails have metamorphosed into filigreed spears of rust. I make the mistake of trying to take hold of one. A shard of rusted metal fragments in my hand, and for the first time I become aware that something about my dream is not quite right. I can feel pain; I can smell something acrid.

I feel sorry for the man I'm shadowing, because although I know he's just a character in my dream, I am experiencing the luxury of sleep whilst he is awake. I am witnessing his apparently endless insomnia.

People boast that dreams are not real, but quantum mechanics tell us that what we call *real* is made up of things which cannot possibly *be* real. My mother faithfully recorded her dreams, in writing, over a period of seventy years. Most people – predominantly men – can't even remember their dreams when they wake. Psychiatrists say that a person suffering from mental illness is less able to recall their dreams than someone who is enjoying good mental health.

Later, I return to the site of the rope bridge. I feel sure that the man will be somewhere in front of me, and there he is! Same hat, same chinos, same vagueness about what's on his feet. This time we're in the riverbed, underneath the rope bridge. He's in front of me, but what's different this time is that I'm aware that I've left some belongings on the opposite riverbank and I've got to get them. Swimming is the only way because a cordon has been put on the rope bridge. Curiously, the man also is returning to the opposite riverbank, so we're both bobbing in the water, him still in front of me.

What I need to recover from the other side of the river is a print-out of something I can't recall at the moment, except I know that it's on pale blue paper – the sort that flyers advertising village fayres are printed on. As we approach the riverbank, another man calls out to me. This is alarming because it's threatening to compromise my secrecy. But the man I'm shadowing seems unaware of my presence, or that of the person who's telling me that he's found the blue paper. I have an awful feeling that the man who's found my paper is police and they're on to me about the telephone call I made.

'We're going to be searching all today,' announces the policeman. That sounds as if they're expecting to find a body in the river, and if they do then it will be my fault because I should have told them who I was when I telephoned. The man in the straw hat – somewhat dripping now – seems oblivious to both myself and the 'policeman' who – I suddenly realise – has addressed me by my name.

In the world of dreams, everybody knows everybody. It's called the 'collective unconscious'. Physicians tell us that sleep is essential, and it's a fact that lack of sleep will lead to death. Vital as sleep is to the human body, sleep gurus tell us that it's a myth that when we are asleep our brains enter hibernation, are at rest, and therefore engaging in a renewal process. The brain, just like the heart and every other organ and bodily system, goes hammering on every second of our lives until we are declared clinically dead. Nightmares are relatively rare. Cognitive experts tell us that bad dreams can be caused by poor mental health, trauma… or by the consumption of toasted cheese at bedtime.

Watching the film called *The Cabinet of Doctor Caligari* is likely to induce a nightmare. The viewer may at first laugh at its funny, dauby, German Expressionist scenery, be irritated by the 1919, flickering, black-and-white photography, be scornful of its quaint subtitles and the histrionic arm movements of its actors. But beware! The ultimate experience is subliminal. Its eponymously named protagonist uses one

of his patients – a somnambulist – to kill people, at random. This – in itself – doesn't seem particularly frightening, but the reason that the film pushes the viewer into the chasm of fear, lies entirely in the context of *what* takes place *where*, and exactly what is revealed in its final scene.

I'm still following the man in the 'straw', picking my way carefully behind him and feeling surprised how wide the river is which we've both just swum. The police are still busy searching, and as I look behind me, I see that the land on the opposite bank of the river is much higher than on our side. Along its crest is a line of large buildings; their domes, finials, and rusticated stone podiums suggest that they are palaces that I should be well acquainted with, that I should have visited them, but I never have.

For the first time, I get the feeling that the man in the straw hat is aware that he's being followed. Every so often he flicks his head to one side. I can see the line of his jaw, his sandy-coloured beard. He reminds me a little of me.

On my side of the river the streets are wide, the buildings low. There are shopping arcades in the form of Arab bazaars and souks. The man glances behind him, and I'm sure he knows I'm tailing him because he avoids looking precisely towards where I am. He steps sideways into one of the market stalls. There are lots of other people, so I can pause without attracting attention, and I casually pick up a decorated pottery lamp from a stall. One of those onion-shaped perforated bowls with a light inside. The stallholder – a man with a forked beard – scrapes his rickety wooden chair backwards over the tiled floor and comes and whispers in my ear. He wants me to look after the stall while he goes to the toilet. I make an excuse because I see that the man with the straw hat has made his way back to the main thoroughfare. I feel guilty at not being prepared to help the stallholder with his inconvenience, but I'm worried that I may lose sight of my man, and despite the fact that I know that this is a dream – at least, I think it is – I feel that there may be consequences if he eludes me.

Back on the main thoroughfare of the arcade, I'm just in time to see my man enter another emporium. This one is selling a variety of men's clothing, and I have an overpowering feeling that I've been here before. It's one of these shops where you can enter through one door, make your way round the counters in a 'U' shape, and leave by another door, so I'm keeping a close eye on Straw Hat. This is quite difficult because the things for sale are very interesting to me. The shop specialises in denim wear but of unusual designs, colour and texture. There's raw and selvedge denim. There are shirts made from fabrics rarely seen on the street: two-tone shot effect, slub weave, and a very fluffy type of flannel. All are neatly folded and displayed behind clear cellophane. I stroke their surfaces with my hand, and the cellophane squeaks, ripples, and catches the light coming from the gently swinging pendants on the ceiling. I touch the cellophane again, this time rubbing my forefinger backwards and forwards to make sure that I'm right about it making that little squeaking sound. I've never been able to do that in a dream before. There are men's ties in similar fabrics: square-ended, narrow, and encased in clear, shiny cellophane. I'm so intent on not losing Straw Hat that I've lost my bearings and doubt if I could find my way here again except by accident. Straw Hat is moving towards the door, so I follow.

Once outside the emporium, I see Straw Hat has quickened his pace. He's probably trying to shake me off. I pass through the doors of the glass-roofed arcade, Straw Hat is no more than a few paces in front of me, and from the feel of the wind on my face and the smell of ozone, I think we are walking towards the sea. I'm correct, and when I see the sea, I'm taken aback by what a perfect colour it is. Aqua water and white sand. The promenade I'm walking along is quite narrow, and because there are so few people, I'm keeping at least twenty yards between me and Straw Hat. The sea looks so flat and such a pretty colour that I can't understand why the concrete beneath my feet is so rough and full of so many holes. The air here can't always be so still and warm. I have to watch my step; a twisted ankle here could have consequences.

The walkway curves to the left, then to the right, so every few seconds I lose sight of Straw Hat. The path is getting narrower, and the concrete rampart on my right so high that I'm starting to be anxious about where I'm being drawn, and whether I'll be able to get back to where I need to be. But I remember, I know this place, it's a travel interchange and I recollect there's a huge cave in the cliff, lined with polished concrete, and two glass elevators which pass through a vertical tunnel cut into the rock. At the top you can get a tram back to the city.

When I arrive at the entrance to the cave, I see that Straw Hat is not there. An ascending elevator has just left, so he must be in it. I wait for the return of that elevator, or its twin, and find that I'm the only person standing in the hall. I tap with my white officer's deck shoes on the hard and shiny floor. When the elevator arrives, it's empty. Its doors slide open and in I go. The doors close and the elevator noiselessly rises, passing through the rock roof of the hall. I notice the strata of years, the attitudes of the rocks, their strike, their bedding planes, all thrusting in the direction of somewhere important. Above me is a space which is filled with blinding sunlight.

My elevator car slows at the platform, and even before its glass doors open, I can see Straw Hat. He's standing facing me, as if waiting for the elevator car, but as I step out, he makes no attempt to walk past me. Just stands there. I can feel him staring *at* me, into my eyes.

Behind me is the aqua sea, and above me a brilliant blue sky. But it's not cloudless, there *are* clouds – stratus, cumulus, cirrus – and I don't need to look up to see them because I can see them reflected in Straw Hat's eyes, in his irises, exactly like a painting I once saw.

But as I look closely, I realise that I'm wrong. I'm not seeing the clouds reflected in his irises, because I am inside his head looking out at the clouds. I am Straw Hat. So, where and who, is the man I thought was me?

Quantum physicists say that reality sometimes defies common sense. Philosophers ask the question, how can we be sure about the boundaries between asleep and awake?

I must be firm, I must be firm. Think of Alice. 'A pinch usually does the trick.' But at variance with Alice's assured indignance, I'm feeling anxious, and it occurs to me that if I am Straw Hat, then the person who I thought I was, will

logically now be in pursuit of me. I can see no other people, so I quicken my pace.

In front of me there is a tram about to depart for the city. I see the twin elevator rising, drawing level with the platform, and I don't need anybody to tell me who is in that elevator. I have to get away, so I run towards the tram. I'm making a surprising amount of noise, deck shoes slapping polished concrete, chinos and cheesecloth rustling and rubbing. I make it to the tram, run down the platform to the last car and hurl myself into it just as the doors are hissing shut. I try to settle on one of the shiny, red, plastic seats, can feel my heart going like hell. I peer into the first tramcar, can see a figure – yes, can see a figure: straw hat, chinos, cheesecloth. I touch hat, he touch hat.

Normally this would be the moment when I wake upon a dewy pillow, making funny yodelling noises, like a boy who's struggling his way through puberty. But no such thing is happening. Instead I feel my teeth clenched in the kind of nervous excitement one might experience having recently ingested some drug. I have ceased to be the hunter and have now become the hunted.

'Reality is unknowable', so, let's have none of this 'I know what I know' stuff, or, 'I don't know much about philosophy, but I know what I believe'. *Do* we interact with people in our dreams – in fact, how much control do we have over our lives when we are awake? Straw Hat and I are engaged in some unidentifiable form of communication. Einstein had a phrase for the phenomenon: 'spooky action at a distance'. There's even a formula for it: $P(a,c) - P(b,a) - P(b,c) \leq 1$

What's really bugging me, is that every time I move, Straw Hat – or that *wannabe* doppelganger who is sitting in the tram car in front – copies me. Scratch under *my* straw, and I see *his* hand go to *his* head. Turn my head to look out of the tram window at the car washes and amusement arcades flashing by, and I see *his* head turn. I need to shake this guy, if it's the last thing I do. I've also realised in the last few moments, something about my predicament which I would prefer not to contemplate further, but I think that sooner or later I may have to.

Out of the window I see a building, a concrete tower block. I have a feeling that is where I live – I say feel, because I cannot be sure, I don't actually know. I have an inkling that this building will offer me sanctuary. The tram is slowing.

When the tram halts, I get off and walk quickly towards the tower block, and I don't need to look behind me to know who is following. Entering the building involves no ceremony other than pulling a handle on the aluminium-framed door, which sticks slightly as I grasp it. Once inside the entrance lobby, I had expected to experience a feeling of home-at-last familiarity. Instead, my anxiety levels are soaring, and I'm perspiring heavily. I try to calm myself, take a breath through my nose. The smell in the lobby is a mixture of popcorn and garlic.

I remember that I live on the top floor, next to the elevator motor room. I know that because I recall lying in bed being able to hear the gentle whirring of the lift motor. I glance back through the entrance door, catch sight of the straw-hatted imposter, and notice that he, too, is wearing officer's deck shoes. The elevator is here. I step in, enjoying a modicum

of confidence that by the time the cheesecloth pretender has reached my floor I will be safe behind my front door.

I press the top floor button. The journey is so quiet and without vibration, that I begin to worry that the car isn't moving, and that when the doors open, I will be confronted by my impersonator. I'm sweating buckets. How often do we perspire in our dreams? We do when we wake up and find ourselves lying on sodden sheets, but my cheesecloth shirt is soaking right now, and every hair on my body feels like it's standing on end.

The lift car comes to a stop, doors open. It's the correct floor because I see my front door, remember the number. The elevator lobby is full of sunlight coming from the window behind me, and as I feel in my right pocket for my key, I hear the tap-tap of officer's deck shoes coming up the emergency stairs. I pull out my key, but my hand is so sweaty I drop the key. It pings on polished concrete. I bend, pick up the key, and as I raise my eyes I see clouds – stratus, cumulus, cirrus – and I don't need to look further to see them because I can see them reflected in *his* eyes, in his irises, exactly like a painting I once saw. But as I look closely, I realise that I'm wrong. I'm not seeing the clouds reflected in his irises, because I am inside his head looking out of the window at the clouds. I am my own imposter. So, where and who, is the man I thought was me?

I hear the tap-tap of officer's deck shoes descending the emergency stairs, and once again I am compelled to follow. As I take the first few steps of my inevitable pursuit, I am conscious of something which I have feared and suspected for some time – that ineluctably, I am not dreaming, I am awake.

THE HIDDEN APARTMENT

I t's getting dangerously near dawn.

'The views are breath-taking! Even at night.'

'You've been saying that all evening, Rory.'

'I'm enjoying the fact that you, Pascal/e, accomplished realtor as you may be, spend your life hugging the ground in that attenuated pseudo-hacienda of yours, whilst I perch ceremoniously twenty-six storeys above the lake – I mean look, look at the light on that water!'

'Lake Shore Drive, LSD! A different block could have got you a whole lot higher than twenty-six.'

'I didn't want higher, I wanted Mies van der Rohe.'

'Oooh, let me remind you, if it wasn't for me, Roo darrling, you wouldn't be here at all.'

'You know perfectly well it was all down to Trista. She was hip to the fact that the Oldbergs wanted to sell, long before they instructed.'

'You know, Rory, I'm flabbergasted to hear you actually

give that girl credit for once. She may be a newbie, but she's a damn good worker. Sixth sense, I'd say.'

'I don't want to heap praises too high; I *am* married to her.'

'We hadn't noticed! So, where *is* Trista?'

'Somewhere? There's such a crowd!'

Being Rory is the ultimate. It means being head and shoulders above everyone else, literally and in all his state of gingerness. It means multi-talent. It means awards, accolade, a transition from deejay, to art historian, and TV presenter to real estate developer in zero to fifty years. It means adulation, and it means not just a towering body; it means a libido of colossal scale. He's a testosterone-filled hubris bubble, and this occasion is his birthday, or is it Christmas? There *are* lights, pink and green, hanging against the full-height windows, and so tiny, that they don't grab the eye so that guests miss the water breaking in white dabs, a mile out on the lake.

Or is it his – sorry, *their* – house-warming? For one moment, he can't remember, but hey! It's three celebrations rolled into one, and quite a do. There's mulled wine, cocktails, cherries. There're caterers – female, *of course*, dressed as Nubian slaves (to Rory type specification) serving canapes and tapas from palm-sized trays of slate and cedar wood. Rory inhales deeply, searching – not for the oral stimulation of dates and marinated pork – but with a finger, in a haptic exploration of Janine's – 'It is Janine, isn't it?' – waist, just above her shapely bottom. Big eyes turn towards Rory. 'Fulsome breasts,' he hears himself mutter. It's a reunion as well, there're folk Rory hasn't seen for years.

'Rory – you, old dog!'

'Feodor!'

'You were the best!' Feodor swishes his pigtail and both his oversized hands grip one of Rory's freckled forearms. 'Five-star in our year at art history graduate school, and the most outrageous TV presenter I ever saw.' Rory smiling – but not *too* much. 'Holy shit! That time you interviewed Frances and the Machine in front of that Venetian portrait… Recounted the story of the Venice syphilis epidemic. You were *so* close you were practically licking her neck. It was a presenter's triumph!'

'Good you could come! Feo. *This*, is a Mies van der Rohe' – pronounces it MeesvandaRower – he takes a sip of his cocktail.

'You named a cocktail after him, great!'

'*No*, the building, man! It was all square rooms, we ripped them out—'

'We?'

'Trista—'

'I didn't know you'd *married* again, Rory.' Rory can just make out above the din beyond Feodor's left ear: '*She's cute, but she's a substitute. His last one killed herself…*'

Rory considers going and grabbing the motherfucker, but he's keen to show Feo the apartment, so settles for mouthing a, '*I'm the kind of guy people love to hate.*'

'*…yeah, killed herself. So did the daughter – daughter wasn't his… everybody that guy comes into contact with…*' Man with a hipster beard.

Rory mouths again, '*Asshole!*'

'*…do you know, he's fathered more children than Genghis Khan.*' Woman wearing a pashmina scarf.

'*Don't tempt me, lady!*' This time *several* heads turn. Feodor is fiddling with his pigtail, pretending not to notice.

It's too late, the pashmina woman spits at Rory. Rory's man – black tuxedo, black shirt – swings in out of nowhere, pinions the woman's arms, levers her away, but not before Rory spits back. Rory is surprised how quick off the mark Pascal/e is with the tissues. Not for dealing with Rory's bespattered psychedelic shirt, but in removing his saliva from the woman's cheek and hurrying away.

'There's this huge wall of glass, which means you can see the lake, all the time. Even from the sleeping area.'

'No overlooking then?'

'No overlooking. Yeh, pity, I enjoy being in the public eye. Doesn't the act of performing appeal to you, Feo? I'm sure I recall at least *one* occasion when it did!' Rory turns full circle, smiling, as if all hundred and something guests are looking at him.

'Is Trista *around*?' The coloured lights begin their cycle of pulsing, the gentle twelve-tone sounds of Terry Riley's 'In C' are marginally audible behind the human hubbub.

'Somewhere, hiding probably. Look! I want to show you – if we can squeeze past these *lervely* people.' Feodor reaches for dark grapes, snatches from the quivering cluster, and – to get into the spirit of the occasion – holds them aloft, skins still cloudy from chilling – tilts his head and pops them into his moist, fleshy mouth. Rory's hand vanishes behind Kelly's waist – 'It is Kelly, isn't it? You can see from one end of the apartment to the other. All the screens are glass.' It's true, it's an internal landscape of light and movement, and the first time Rory has seen it full of people, all enjoying its undulating shimmering drifts of colour.

'Trista's always talking about the window cleaners. They go up and down on these trapezes, wiping the glass.

"Shouldn't we have a bit more privacy, Rory?" she says. Loosen up, girl! She's quite a bit younger than me. "Roar?" she asks. "Should we be having those lower windows open like that – particularly when it's freezing outside? Those guys could squeeze right in." We should be so lucky, says I. "Just chill, will you, hon, and turn up the heating. I'm a believer in conspicuous consumption.'"

'Pascal/e! So, wha'd'ya think...?' Pascal/e reappears, swivelling his/her tightly-cream-trousered hips to negotiate an elderly, bald male in meaningful huddle with a twenty-something leotarded female. '...Age shall know no boundaries.'

'Well, it certainly doesn't with you, dear.' Rory can feel the gentle resistance of the poured-rubber floor beneath his espadrilles, can sense the wool of Pascal/e's cream Nehru jacket as he takes hold of it with left thumb and finger, can smell vanilla, sandalwood. He can also feel with his right hand the derriere of Serena – 'It is Serena, isn't it?'

'It's the free city of the mind, Pascal/e. Hasn't anyone told you? Oh, this is Feo – art history graduate school.' Cocktails switch from right hands to left, and Feodor crushes, while Pascal/e strokes. There's a trace of artificial ceremony between the two of them, as if they've met before. 'So, what do you think of the apartment? I'm dying for your opinions.'

'Ooh, sheer architectural poetry, Roo darrling.' Rory beams.

'It's unique. You've done a fantastic job!' Feodor.

'Where *is* Trista?' Both.

'Somewhere she's *so* petite, and this crowd – she could be anywhere.'

Blasé, Rory may sound. But this persistent questioning

on the whereabouts of Trista reminds him that *something* has happened – just the other day – which is troubling him deeply. It's a thing so unusual that, standing here in the normality of the mass of guests, talking to Pascal/e and Feodor, he finds it almost impossible to believe. For one uncouth moment he considers telling his friends, because what *has* happened would make a great dinner-party anecdote, admirable cabaret, but he's – and perhaps wisely so – unable to share. Even with Trista; in fact, most of all with Trista.

A hole has appeared in the wall of the apartment. A rough-shaped hole. Concrete blocks have been removed from near the entrance to their apartment. It leads into the next apartment. No one can see the hole because it's hidden behind an armoire which stands against the neighbouring wall. The hole was not there the day Rory and Trista moved into the apartment; it appeared after the armoire was placed against the wall.

'*Ah!*' say Pascal/e and Feodor in unison as the mass of folk behind them split apart. Then Rory sees *her* coming – out of nowhere, it seems, and with that very slight inclination of the head. She's smiling. Some say she carries an aura; perhaps, but Rory tries to insist to himself that the haze behind her is coming from a hotplate where a tall and torqued chef is conjuring prawns flambé and bananas foster. Aura or no, Rory has a sense that he's known Trista, long ago, in another world. He's almost overcome with a feeling of relief to see her, yet, he can't resist bowling a brickbat: 'Trist, must you *hide* all the time? You know, you really need to loosen up, start letting your hair down, girl!

The tempo changes from twelve-tone to 4/4. It's the only way for Rory, it *has* to be 120 beats per minute. He *must* create the honey which attracts the bees. 'I Feel Love'! He feels love! Rory begins to dance, but not Trista.

It was like sex. Every time he did it, it was just that little bit different – visiting the hidden apartment that was. His first thought, when he discovered the hole in the wall, was to tell Trista. But as he climbed into what seemed to be the neighbouring apartment, he was seized with a conviction that this was *his* find, and he was gripped with a desire to keep it for himself.

The mystery apartment was identical in layout to their own. Full-height windows overlooking the lake, and equally spacious, but stark-staring empty. Bare concrete floor, no internal walls, no kitchen, no bathroom fittings; just plumbing pipes for a future owner to fix into. Of course, he would buy it, knock down the rest of that wretched block wall. His property would be the size of a nightclub! But an unseen voice was insisting that this was special; it would be his secret space, *his* alone. Every angle, every shadow, every trick of the light, seemed charged with exclusive but elusive meaning.

Rory walked over to the door, tried it; it was locked. As he turned back to face the windows, he saw that there were pictures hanging on the wall – six, perhaps, small and in ornate gilt frames. Reproductions, and unsurprisingly, he recognised several. The rites of spring, bacchanalian subjects with writhing semi-clothed figures wearing wreaths of vine leaves, brandishing drinking vessels. How absurd! It seemed as if someone had put them there solely for him – but he *would* think that. Trista thought he had an ego the size of the universe... Never said – not with her lips, but he wasn't such an infant as not to read the signals. Neither had he been so stupid as not to get the message from Zoya. It wasn't his fault she killed herself. He played around, had affairs, couldn't help it. It was the way he was made. Sure, he could understand Trista's reluctance to experiment – he'd suggested a threesome, foursomes. Black girls were loose, that's what he'd heard some time ago, but it was a myth… In fact, they were very, *very* proper. Maybe she *was* beginning to loosen up, trying to tell him something, and this was the way she was getting her message across. For Christ's sake! Trista couldn't have put these pictures here, made the hole in the wall. That was insane thinking. But he would damn well find out who did.

Rory's first visit to the Hidden Apartment had been brief – no more than minutes. He hadn't wanted Trista waking up, wondering where he was, finding the hole. The day after the party there was no chance for a forensic investigation because Trista was working from home, the two of them supervising contract cleaners he'd hired to get the place back to rights. But the following day Trista and Pascal/e had a client meeting out of town. Perfect! Rory stood staring at the armoire, a repulsive piece – Russian, evidently, and alien to *his* future-modernist interior, but its survival was an act of faith in memory of Trista's great-grandparents. Rory fiddled the crudely fashioned key into the lock, turned, and the door creaked open.

Jesus, what a day the move in had been! The armoire had been in store, so it was the storemen who'd brought it to site in its various parts, put it together, and fixed it to the wall. Bosie and Ludie, what a pair! Pascal/e recommended them;

thought they were great. They weren't; they were congenital idiots. Identical blue denim bib and braces, they looked like Okies from a John Steinbeck, but their performance was undiluted Laurel and Hardy. They got the goddamned thing in position, assembled the parts; there was banging and hammering from hell. Then they left.

Ten minutes later: 'It's Bosie… Left my phone, calling on Ludie's.'

'Can't see it anywhere.'

'It's inside *that* closet…'

'Armwaarr!'

'Behind it… You have to take out the back panel.'

'Hold on, I'm inside the armoire right now, taking out the back panel… Jesus, fuck!'

'What?' Rory could see the phone, nestling in the half inch of air between the back panel and the wall. He could also see right into the next apartment, and on either side of him – rough and ragged, and ineluctably gaping – was the mother of holes.

'What the fuck have you guys done!'

'What?' There was a pathetic whine in Bosie's voice. Sure, the two of them had made one hell of a racket, but they couldn't have done this. It was a sledgehammer job; what had happened to the blocks which had been removed? Something made Rory ask no more questions.

'Ya phone's here, come get!'

Rory climbed into the armoire, closed the door behind him. Could smell polish, waxes, old dusters, the baize on which had stood generations of porcelain. He fumbled with the back panel. Off it came in his hands and daylight from the mystery apartment invaded the inside of the

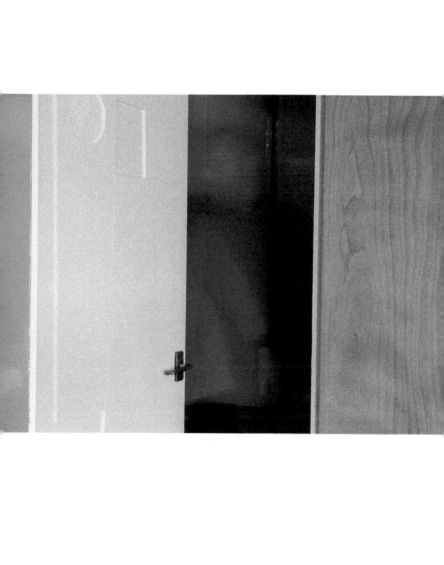

armoire. There it was; the hole was still there. It was like goddamned Narnia!

Rory breathed deeply. His nostrils tingled with the rawness of smashed concrete; his hand felt the grit of mortar fragments as he climbed through the hole. It was silent in the Hidden Apartment after the scraping noises he'd made inside the armoire, his espadrilles soundless against the concrete floor. Through the windows he could see giant mounds of cloud hanging over the lake – as if the scene had acquired a winter mountain scape during the night. The apartment was full of light and there were dust motes shining and drifting from ceiling to floor. But it had been two days since the hole had been made; it should have settled by now. Something made Rory wheel round and look towards the main apartment door; someone had just left. He ran to it, grabbed, pulled; it was locked.

He was surprised at his own feeling of relief at finding himself alone. As a celebrated lover of the human race, he sometimes found it difficult to comprehend how much he enjoyed solitude. On his own with objects, at one with the very fabric of his surroundings. Childhood trauma so often put up barriers between people in later life. His mother's depression, his own shameful wetting of the bed right up until the night before he was sent away to boarding school. There'd been the business with Zoya. Everybody blamed him for that. She'd wanted a divorce. She'd called it 'mental cruelty'; the attorney she'd hired said it was 'psychological abuse'. Either way, she didn't want to go through with it. Lack of staying power, or maybe something to do with the fact that she was adopted. He almost sympathised with her.

Then, it was the daughter, *her* daughter. Everybody

blamed him for that, as well. He'd never had time for little Sophia, couldn't be bothered, except he'd been dimly aware that she'd been popular, lots of friends – close to one in particular, cute little black girl.

He began to focus on the pictures… Couldn't be sure, but he could have sworn they were hung in a different order from when he'd seen them two days ago. William Etty's 'Before the Flood' had been next to Poussin's 'A Bacchanalian Revel', he was certain of it. He looked closer – after all, his examination of the pictures was of a professional nature; it was more than the mere satisfying of a sordid curiosity. Voices? Probably out in the corridor. Pascal/e, out of town, but supposing it was one of his/her assistants coming to do a viewing? It would be embarrassing to be caught in the empty apartment and looking at what might be regarded as naughty pictures. The voices faded, the door remained closed, and Rory continued his perusing.

At first, he'd thought they were reproductions; closer scrutiny told him they were originals, and in high-quality gilt frames, nicely distressed. Etty's 'Before the Flood' contained certain aspects of authenticity, but overall it was bogus, artificially aged. There was no doubt it was a copy of Etty; that lubricious-looking female, centre foreground, big eyes, turned upwards towards the viewer, and leaning backwards ever so slightly to emphasise the curve of her bottom, and whatever else she'd got, Jesus! Rory's face was so close he was practically licking the painting. More voices? Fading away; all clear. There were swarthy and bearded Romani characters too; it was all arms, hands, legs, in one swaying, grasping, circular mass. An emphasis on dark skin, as if the painter – or those of his era – believed that dark skin was somehow predatorial. Rory stepped back. There was Bacchus and Ariadne by Poussin, a Brueghel; who had done these? A forger? This little display had the hallmark of Pascal/e, s/ he had fingers in lots of pies, and without doubt some of them dodgy. Rory had never trusted Pascal/e. Trista said that was being prejudiced again trans people, but even as his suspicion intensified, it softened. After all, it was Pascal/e who'd introduced him to Trista. Head-hunted her from Fizzcox Insurance: 'This is my new assistant, Trista.' Christ! She was a black Sally Bowles, and gorgeous! He couldn't believe his luck, and even more so when *she* proposed, and no more than a matter of days later.

A thought. That crudely fashioned key to the armoire. Rory remembered he'd left it in the door of the armoire, which had a nasty habit of creaking its way open. Supposing Trista were to return early, discover it open, see the hole. Or even worse, merely shut the door without looking and lock it. He would be a prisoner. He had sated his lust over the paintings sufficiently for one day; now he would start making enquiries of his own. He was damned if he was going to ask Pascal/e about this. If Pascal/e wanted to play games with him, Rory would ignore them.

Apartment #102. Rory hovered outside, still in two minds as to whether or not to tell anyone about his discovery. The bell sounded 'Hi Ho Silver Lining'. There was a long interval as he shifted about on his espadrilles. While *he* looked up and down the corridor, he had the distinct feeling that he was being eyed through the spyhole. The door clicked open. A man of about thirty was standing there, sideways, as if he was engaged in some more important activity with an unseen person. He looked like a man about to fight a duel.

'Hi, Rory from number 104, just moved in.' The man – shoulder-length black, curly hair, moustache, impressively tanned skin – was dressed in a white singlet and grey tracksuit bottoms. He was snarling, as if at an enemy. '…oh, and Trista.' At this information, the snarl turned into a leer.

'…Don't suppose you know who lives at number 103?'

'Empty.' It was a desultory sound, like that made by a man in a bar whilst nodding towards a dead beer glass.

'Didn't catch your name?'

'Louis!' It came in an aggressive rush of sound like a dog-walker calling his pet.

'Ignore Bacchus at your peril, it's a part of yourself that you must acknowledge.'

It was afterwards. Rory always felt like this *afterwards*. As if Trista somehow hadn't tried hard enough and he'd been left, abandoned in a kind of limbo. He was lying on his back, hands clasped behind head, his ginger curls flopping sideways as if they were an extra pair of ears. He couldn't help talking about Bacchus; he also felt an urge to tell about the Hidden Apartment and its secrets, but somehow, he knew he must resist. Trista had become a silent shape under the black satin duvet, a portion of her thigh just visible, and Rory could see the birthmark which had always nearly driven him crazy. Who said black people didn't have birthmarks? They were bluish. The shape under the duvet began to utter, '"For any sort of perception or creation to exist, a certain psychological precondition is essential… intoxication," Nietzsche…' Rory felt a surge of pride; statements like this were pudding proof that she wasn't stupid – she'd majored in philosophy – but

more so because it showed that she actually *got* what he was about; even if he didn't really feel that she was his equal. '…
If people had acknowledged the need to indulge Bacchus, then we wouldn't have had the Vietnam War!'

'I was too young.'

'Nobody is too young for war.'

Rory lay there. He couldn't understand how one so petite could produce such loud snoring. No wonder so many couples had separate rooms. But Rory didn't believe in rooms, walls, doors. They were barriers, boxes, categories; he hated all that. The world was one; it was one, was one, one…

'There were some men in the apartment.'

'What, window cleaners? You should be so lucky!'

'No, listen, Roar, it was a dream, *so* vivid.'

'There were two guys, fit, looked like they worked out – and another guy, black curly hair, snarly face. They had vine leaves in their hair. I'm not sure if I should tell you more.' Trista was giggling.

'Was I there?' Rory couldn't resist the question.

'No, I don't think you were.'

Rory had had a bad night. He'd lain awake a long time. Had paced the apartment, seen the light on the lake, felt the squeak of his finger against the leather banquette seating, and examined the sticky stain on the Noguchi glass coffee table, which the contract cleaners had missed. He'd returned to bed, hands behind ginger head, elbows pointing towards the lake, and as sullen as hell. Those paintings, they were probably still there, and no more than a few feet away on the other side of the wall. He would have another look this morning. Trista was in the office all day with Pascal/e, while once again for Rory, the day was his.

From the moment he crawled inside the armoire, he could sense a change. Someone, or something, had been here. He thought he could smell the faintest trace of incense, or was it his imagination? Russian Orthodox? The goddamned thing had *come* from Russia, along with Trista's grandmother after World War Two before the Cold War really caught a hold. Oh, *yes*! There *were* black families in Russia – came from Africa after the Revolution. When he first met Trista, he'd thought it was a hell of a coincidence that Zoya had been Russian.

He prised off the back panel, and the armoire took on the uneasy half-light of a partly submerged chapel. He stretched his legs through the hole, onto the concrete floor, and as he looked towards the lake, he felt again that batting of wings in his stomach as he saw the sparkle of dust particles. He hadn't disturbed that dust. Someone else had been here. A trace of vanilla, sandalwood? He leaped to the door; once again, it was locked.

He was sure the pictures were different. N.D. Beauvais, he recognised at once. An engraving, Bacchanalian Gathering with Leopards Pulling; an apparently docile leopard pulling a cart bearing a massive urn packed with grapes. Figures – male and female, vine-leafed, clutching drinking vessels, and each other. A supine, half-clothed female figure in a swoon, a male figure with powerful sternohyoid neck and, piercing his right ear, a pearl ear stud. He'd written an essay on this engraving at graduate school. Rory thought back to the party. What the hell *had* Feodor been doing in town anyway? He couldn't remember inviting him? He hadn't seen him in *years*.

He moved to the next picture, Poussin's 'A Bacchanalian Revel' – again, a mass of half-robed, vine leaf-headed figures groping each other. A female, a male arm round her neck in what could be an act of strangulation were it not for the look of rapture on her face. A man, centre right, bearded, and tattooed. Next! Christ! This one wasn't there before. He felt a tingling of excitement, shock and lust. It was a pen-and-ink drawing in the style of Picasso's late 'bull and satyr' series. Whilst the salaciousness of the other works was no more than an implication, the content of the drawing in front of him left nothing to the imagination. The drawing showed a female being pleasured by a stocky curly-haired moustachioed male. She seemed to be enjoying the experience, while he was snarling. In the foreground was the figure of a black slave girl, seated in what might be interpreted as a submissive pose – the head inclined away from the scene of copulation. The slave girl was wearing a subucula, drawn up to her thighs. The birthmark he knew so well was just visible.

Rory's shaking hand pulled the framed drawing from the wall, where it had been hung on wire and screw. He rummaged for signature, any clue as to who might have done this. Provenance, look at the back! He turned it over, let out a nervous laugh. Over the surface of the brown gummed paper someone had written the word 'AMOIRE'. It was crudely done, in red ink and brush, probably while the frame had been held in a vertical position, thus allowing the ink to run down from the letters as if someone had wanted it to look like blood.

Rory could feel the start of panic. He needed more information. He lifted the pictures from their hooks, turning each in his hands, but there were no more cryptic inscriptions. He replaced them, took a deep breath, ran his hand through his ginger curls, and hurried towards the hole in the wall. As he clumped his way back through the armoire, he glanced nervously about him as if expecting more messages to emerge from its encrusted woody interior. He thumped the door shut and locked it, as if this simple physical act would exorcise any demons which were lurking within. He looked around him, stood stock still, then let out a guffaw. Of course! There had been no 'r' between the 'a' and the 'm'. Whoever had written it had meant *amour* – 'love'! It was obvious, and it had clearly been written by an idiot. He shouted aloud in relief, 'Howdy doody, lickety-split!' He thumped the rubber floor with each of his espadrilles in turn and high-fived an imaginary person.

'Just supposing…' Rory began. Trista raised one eyebrow – she was good at doing that. '…supposing there was an apartment, exactly like this one, but it had secrets?' It was a kind of boast, he knew it. Trista was sitting cross-legged on a small mound of black satin.

'I'd say that you were in danger of straying into Jungian metaphysics.' Given the vagueness of his question, it sounded like an appropriately guarded answer… a slick one, anyway. She didn't believe him. For one moment he wondered if he should grab her hand, pull her to the armoire, and show her the goddamned hole.

'Should we buy it, the apartment?' His voice sounded boyishly enthusiastic.

'You're the acquisitive one, I just do the negotiating.'

To give men's minds wings, give men's minds wings, men's minds wings, minds wings, wings…

Rory opened one eye, could see Trista sitting up, alert. She lifted herself off the bed, on palms of hands; rocked backwards and forwards, shook her head, and gave him a chinny sort of smile. Oh God, why did she seem so familiar? Eartha Kitt, that was it. Sitting there, she looked just like Eartha. 'I had another dream.'

'The window cleaners,' he murmured, like he'd heard it a thousand times.

'Noow.' She sounded as if she were issuing a restraining order to a small child. There was the slight forward inclination of the head. Rory could feel the bat wings in his stomach. 'It was the same three guys... wearing loincloths.' She giggled. 'You look worried.'

'No, go on.'

'...Very dark-skinned – maybe Italian. Another guy with a big beard, and muscular neck – oh, and a pearl ear stud.' The bat wings beat more strongly in Rory's stomach and he felt his buttocks tingle.

'What were they doing?' He couldn't help himself.

'Mmm, not a lot; the guys in the loincloths were strutting around – quite funny, and... there were other people here.'

'Here? You mean, in this sleeping area?'

'I think so.'

'Who?'

'I think Pascal/e... and that friend of yours who was at the party.'

'Which friend?'

'The one with the pigtail who kept slapping you on the back.'

'*Feodor?*' Rory's voice sounded surprised.

'Probably.' She laughed again. 'They were wearing togas. Pascal/e looks really good in a toga.'

'I can imagine.'

'The masters were wearing togas, the slaves wearing loincloths. That's the way it was.' She had an alarming way of making it sound as if she knew something more. 'Slaves were a resource… they always have been, right the way down through time, and in more ways than you can imagine.'

'What were *you* wearing?'

'Oooh, that *would* be telling.'

It was the office again for Trista; Rory stayed home. He was torn between calling a builder, getting the hole blocked up, or simply ignoring the whole damn thing. But it didn't feel like a choice. To block up the hole would be almost like shutting off a part of himself – his personality. He would wait, see what happened. He had other things to get on with. He switched on his computer, but opening emails had somehow had lost its attraction; something else was pulling at him. He would go to the apartment, have another look at those pictures, see if there was anything more to learn.

It was with a degree of relief when he stepped through the hole that he saw that the pictures had gone. He padded over to the wall and looked closely. There were no small holes. They'd all been on hangers screwed into the white plaster wall; he was sure of it. He stood back in disbelief, thought he could hear a noise, the click of fingers?

A half-seen form, way over against the opposite wall adjacent to the windows. A transient spectre; was he imagining this as well? As Rory stared, a shape peeled itself away from the white wall, which a moment ago it had seemed to be part of. Freestanding, solid, and of human appearance, it stood silhouetted against the windows. The lake-cloud beyond gave the impression of being piled around it, as if it were a precious figurine nestling in a gift box. Rory did not move. It was as if his powers of locomotion had been stolen and given to this *thing*, this section of plaster wall which had diabolically been given life.

The figure took several steps towards him, turned full circle, and Rory could see that it was human, male, and wearing a white mask. It was naked except for a white loincloth and was covered from head to foot in white body paint, the head wreathed in white vine leaves, and like an animal in the wild under threat, its mouth formed into a snarl.

'You bastard!' Fear was fuelling Rory. As he closed on the charade player, he could see Rory had the height advantage, but the white figure was muscular. Left hand – yank away his loincloth and at the same time kick with his right foot! Rory never made it, a burst of hand-clapping stopped him like a gunshot, made him look right where a few feet away a second figure had sprung from a similar state of seclusion. An arpeggio of triumphant laughter from Rory's left, and a third figure lurched into view. The newcomers were white-painted and naked. Being clothed seemed to give Rory no psychological advantage. Unabashed, the two naked men strutted backwards and forwards, wangs a-wagging. It was terrifyingly comic. Then, in a concerted act of menace the three men closed in. Rory glimpsed moustache, beard, sternohyoid neck, pearl ear stud, and a tattoo. He thought he would faint, but the men broke, while Rory – his espadrilles childishly slapping the concrete and his arms flailing in front of him – fled through the hole to safety.

Out of the armoire and in the warm, glassy normality

of his own apartment, Rory poured himself a Scotch and sat down at his computer. He would call the police – no, that wouldn't work; he would call a builder, get that goddamned hole blocked up. A new icon caught his attention on his Google page: 'ANCESTRY DNA'. Out of sheer nervous reflex, he clicked on it. '*Your DNA results*' …he didn't recall requesting them. Clicked again: '*60% North American, 34% Scottish, 2% English, 4% European*'. Hmm, not uninteresting. He looked at the searches: '*over 300 relatives*'. Yeah, they would all be sixth cousins; he'd heard all about this. There were second cousins – two located in the same city. Then his eye went to the top – children, *his* children, children he didn't know about. Five of them! Names; three girls, two boys. He recognised some of the surnames; others he'd never seen before. Jesus Christ! He'd sowed enough wild oats in his time to feed a fucking army, yes, but who had done this? How? Someone had been doing a *lot* of research, a lot of planning, and a lot of persuasive whispering had gone on in a lot of ears. It was Pascal/e, wasn't it? He recalled that altercation when he'd spat at the woman wearing the pashmina scarf. Yes, Pascal/e, hurrying away with his saliva on a tissue. He would go sort that guy, for good, right now.

Rory dodged into the dressing area, reached inside the closet. Pulled a black leather Bergman bomber which left its hanger dithering on the metal rail. Car keys, apartment keys; he locked it. Why? Half the fucking block could get into this apartment, it seemed. He slammed the door, pussy-footed along the carpet, and called the elevator. Got out at the basement car park.

Everything seemed loud after the silent, soft-coloured

glassiness of his apartment, and it dawned on him that he hadn't been outside for five days. The booming and echoing which thundered off the walls and roof of the concrete park filled him with a different kind of anxiety. He unlocked, got in the car, pressed the starter for longer than was necessary, producing a sound like a distressed chihuahua. It was the kind of squealing which he imagined would shortly be coming out of Pascal/e. He pulled out of the car park, wound the window down, and a rush of biting air invaded the car interior. Everything felt unreal out here; he was already wanting to be back in his haven on the twenty-sixth floor. Even the Hidden Apartment possessed a reality preferable to this; it was as if there was an inexplicable kind of safety concealed within its danger. He wasn't going kill Pascal/e – he would scare him/her; that would do for now.

Fullerton Avenue, Fullerton Parkway, on to Lakeshore. Why was he driving north? He should be heading south for town. The fact was, he didn't know what he was actually going to say to Pascal/e. 'Nice little show you put on for me back there, Pascal/e!' It wouldn't do – plus, there'd be Trista hanging around. What was *she* going to think? The two of them seemed to have acquired an uncannily close relationship. No, he was stymied – best go back, wait and see how things developed. Violence – even threats of it would be bound to work against him. They always had done in the past.

As Rory entered the elevator car, he was surprised to find he was sharing it with two men. Apart from Louis, he hadn't seen any other residents. He was amused to note that each was wearing an identical white tee shirt, grey tracksuit bottoms, and carrying a small dumbbell in his right hand.

'Floor?' The bearded one spoke.

'Twenty-six.' As the man turned his head to press the button, something flashed in the fluo light. It was a pearl ear stud. The doors closed and the three men were carried noiselessly upwards. The bearded man had not pressed any other numbers.

Rory leaned backwards against the elevator car wall opposite the men. He was fighting the bats flying about in his stomach. Everything was there, all the information he'd asked for but didn't *really* want. The sternohyoid neck, the moustache, the tattoo. It was them, the charade players, the bogus bacchanalians. As the doors opened at level twenty-six, Rory backed out onto the carpet. The men followed him, then turned and headed towards apartment #101. He must speak and break this goddamned spell,

'Hi, we're neighbours. I've just moved in to 104...' No response. The moustachioed man had the key in the door of #101. In a move of desperation, Rory advanced towards the bearded guy with his right hand outstretched. The man carefully placed the dumbbell on the carpet, as if he were reluctantly letting go of a gold ingot, and – with considerably less care – took Rory's hand. Neither men had changed their deadpan expressions. '...Yeah, me and Trista.' A simultaneous and knowing leer spread from one muscular face to the other. The moustachioed man opened the apartment door, turned to Rory, and offered his hand. Dark-skinned, it was one of those hands with a lot of hair on the back of the fingers. Rory had a view into the apartment and the bats in his stomach began flap-flapping off the radar. On the hall table, where a normal person might have placed a mirror, there hung a painting in a heavy gilt frame. It was in the style of Nicholas Poussin's 'A Bacchanalian Revel'.

When Rory opened the door of his own apartment, he was taken aback to find Trista.

'Early!'

'Things good. Whole batch sales just gone through, no more negotiation till Monday!' Jesus! Rory couldn't even remember what day it was. He took off his bomber, returned it to the hanger in the dressing area, glanced into the sleeping area. Jesus Christ!

'Trista!'

'Comeeng.'

'What?' He was pointing at the wall over the head of the bed.

'I thought you'd like it… You look a bit shaken.'

'Ohh noo! Just doing the Watusi.' Sarcastic. His arms were gyrating, legs bending at the knee. It was helping sooth the shock. On the wall, feet away from where they would – hopefully – in a few hours be making love on those soft, black, satin sheets, hung William Etty's 'Before the Flood'. He staggered forward, peered closer. It had been fixed firmly to the wall with artificially aged brass screws. This was a side of Trista's personality he had previously never encountered, and it hit him like a punch in the face how little he actually knew about her.

For the first time in their relationship, Rory found he couldn't do it.

'It doesn't matter, Roar.'

Roar like a lion? He couldn't even get a fucking hard-on! He lay, miserable and confused. Ancestry DNA, that *had* to be Pascal/e, but *these* guys! Toxic Tweedledum, Tweedledee, and Lethal Louis, it wasn't *quite* Pascal/e's style. Maybe there were *two* things going on? Perhaps Trista was the victim of some bizarre residents' coven whose members *had* entered the apartment while Rory had been asleep and taken liberties with his wife. Quite possibly these covert atrocities had been committed in the dead of night – he'd been drugged, that was it! He'd been feeling like death warmed up every morning since the hole had first appeared. But if there were two scenarios, then they still had to be linked by the pictures, and what was all this slave-and-master stuff? The girl had an impossibly lively imagination; nevertheless, he'd seen these tinted ruffianly weightlifters with his own eyes. It was no good – dead of night or not, he had to go visit the Hidden Apartment. It was like a nagging inconvenience.

A lot of men, and some women, keep firearms in their properties – usually stashed in a safe. Thief break in – you have to kill 'em. Not Rory... didn't believe in it. You could smash a nose, break a jaw with a knuckleduster. Rory took his from its hiding place, pulled on chinos, a sweatshirt, and espadrilles for stealth. He took a torch and tiptoed to the armoire, unlocked, climbed in, and shut the door behind him. He squatted there in the pitch dark, listening to his hammering heart and breathing deeply in an attempt to achieve calm. Incense, vanilla, sandalwood? He tremblingly removed the back panel. It was like emerging from a tomb.

Something was very different. The hole was bigger, it was tidier, and when he shone the torch, he saw that its edges had not only been replastered, but a wood doorframe had been fitted. What did it mean? He climbed out of the armoire and walked cautiously through the new doorway. His heart gave an extra hard bang – the pictures were back. There was sufficient moonlight to see their outlines. Yes, they were all there. He shone the torch about him, knuckledustered fist at the ready, expecting the beam to reveal some figure, yet it seemed he was alone. He would examine each picture in turn, would get to the bottom of this, even if it killed him.

He removed the smutty pseudo-Picasso from the wall, curious to once again inspect its reverse inscription with the schoolboy error. He turned it over. The crudely daubed red ink 'AMOIRE' was still there, but holy shit! Someone had inserted an 'R' between the 'A' and the 'M': ARM-O-I-R-E. It was what he'd previously feared: the clue *was* in the armoire. When Trista was away negotiating on Monday, he would examine it – take the goddamned thing to pieces if need be. He hurried through the remainder of the pictures, and it was what was on the reverse of the engraving – 'Bacchanalian Gathering with Leopards Pulling' – which really shook him. Rory shone the torch. There was an A5 sheet of white paper neatly adhering to the brown backing of the picture. At first, he thought it was a circuit diagram – he looked closer; it was a family tree.

The tree was a meticulously printed graphic. It consisted of bubbles which contained the people, and horizontal and vertical lines indicating directions of heredity. The bubbles contained no more than ten names; there *were* more bubbles, but they indicated only a 'M' for male, 'F' for female. Rory could see his own name, partnered with Zoya. A dotted line ran down from his name, beneath which were five bubbles, each giving the names of his five children whom he had learned of yesterday. That left three names, including a line descending from Zoya to the hapless Sophia. Then came two massive shocks. He'd known Zoya was adopted, but here it was; the tree was telling him that Zoya's adopted parents had previously taken on another child – Feodor. Jesus H. Christ, it was the same Feodor; why had he never realised?

The second shock was bigger. *There* was the bubble with Trista's name in it, the vertical line rising to her parents, above that to her grandparents, and away to the right a dotted line. Oh, singing hell! Zoya was the adopted child of Trista's grandparents. Trista was her niece – a kind of niece, anyway, and Sophia a kind of sister. That vision in Rory's mind, Sophia's special little friend, so cute, the black girl. Rory must get to Trista, explain, he hadn't meant to be cruel to Zoya, it just happened, she would understand. He must talk to her, *now*, before that monster Feodor gets to her.

Speed was of the essence. He placed the picture on the floor, turned, ran towards the hole – but of course, it wasn't a hole anymore – he stopped short. When he had entered the apartment, he'd noticed the new doorway, but what he had failed to observe was that a heavy wooden door had been fitted. He hadn't seen it when he came in because it was wide open, flat back against the wall on double-jointed hinges. Maddeningly and mysteriously, it was now shut, and even before he tugged at the handle, he knew it would be locked. He raced to the apartment door, but it too was locked. He was a prisoner.

It was his duty to escape. He must convince Trista that he had always tried his best with Zoya; he *had* to save her from that evil genius Feodor. Again, he shone the torch about him – could he get up onto the roof? A thought came to him as suddenly as if he'd dropped a heavy weight onto the floor. He remembered that he'd left the lower window open in the sleeping area. That's what he would do! He would climb across the outside face of the glass windows, squeeze in, wake Trista, and alert her to the danger. It was no more than a few feet. Rory had climbed in Yosemite; he knew a pinch hold from a jug hold, could tell a sloper from a pocket. It wouldn't be easy, but it would only take a few seconds.

As he made his noiseless way towards the windows, a shape caught his eye on the wall. It was the size of a medal and emitted a pale glow. He felt himself drawn towards it, bent forward and examined. It was a hole. He looked through. He stared, blinked, as he found himself looking into his own sleeping area. He could see the warm light of the glass partitions. The bed was empty, no sign of Trista. His eye could detect movement beyond the screens, the luminous greens, the hot pinks, and something new moving, patches of purple. Of course, the bacchanalian picture had been put there to hide the hole, but why, and by whom?

He reached the window, released the catch as quietly as he could. He calculated; five seconds to squeeze out and gain the first foothold on the window cleaner's steel brackets. Then fifteen seconds to make the three moves across the face of the glass – one foot on bottom bracket, one hand on top bracket – and five further seconds to squeeze in through his own sleeping area window. It was damn cold out there; if he took longer, he would start to lose sensation in his hands. He pocketed the knuckleduster and was in the act of placing the torch on the floor when he became aware of a form against the wall on his right. His head had almost been touching it. He picked up the torch, shone. It was a human figure, dressed in a loincloth, head wreathed in vine leaves, and painted from top to toe in white body paint. Placed around each of its ankles was a flat metal strap, twice bent, drilled, and screwed to the wall. A similar device had been used around each of its upper arms to prevent forward or downward movement. The person was quite dead; it was Pascal/e.

Just visible beneath the body paint on the neck were a number of dark bruises. The work of those massive hands of Feodor; it *had* to be. Poor Pascal/e! Rory regretted having thought so ill of him/her. Pascal/e had done all the legwork on this, dug the dirt on Rory, and, his/her purpose fulfilled, s/he had been relegated to the status of a slave, and cruelly disposed of. But if Pascal/e had been the 'the slave', then who was the 'master'? Rory's mission had become more urgent than ever. In twenty-five seconds, he would be with his wife; he would tell her everything.

Feet first, Rory squeezed out into the stillness of the biting air and gained the first foothold. His face inches from the wall of glass, he could see the moon reflected behind him. He prepared for the first handhold. It was further than he had calculated and he had to stretch his full height, his espadrilled foot straining on tiptoe. Shift body weight, commit move, yay! First stage complete. A loud report almost caused him to let go. His head was facing the way he was going, and he couldn't see behind him, but he knew that sound; it was the noise a window makes when being forcefully shut from inside. Someone had entered the Hidden Apartment and closed it. He pressed on; shift body weight, commit, yay! He'd made the second set of brackets. 'Bang!' This time he could see the source of the sound. The lower window in his own apartment had been shut from inside. There were no options other than to continue with the final move. Shift body weight, commit, yay! He was now directly outside his apartment, one foot perched on the lower steel bracket, one hand stretched above his ginger head and clutching the upper bracket. He must resemble a giant insect which had flown against the glass and was briefly adhering there, stunned, before falling. He was twenty-six storeys above the lake and beginning to shiver. It would be just a matter of time. His face was pressed against the window, and he could feel the glacial pressure on his forehead, his eyebrows; it was squashing his nose, his chin. In an effort to provide moisture and warmth, his mouth had opened, and his tongue was moving against the surface of the glass.

The man outside the window is looking into his own sleeping area where an incomprehensible tableau has been created. On the bed lies a young woman wearing a purple robe which has fallen open at thigh and breast. She is receiving the intimate attentions of three males. They are naked, tanned, muscular; one with beard, sternohyoid neck and pearl ear stud; the second moustachioed and tattooed; the third with snarling mouth. Standing a distance from the bed is a fourth male, pigtailed and wearing a toga, his arm raised in apparent homage to the foursome. Hail Trista, hail Tzar Trista!

The woman is looking straight at the man outside the window. She's smiling. The mouth and tongue on the outside of the glass are struggling to move.

'Trista, help me, PLEASE!'

For exclusive discounts on Matador titles,
sign up to our occasional newsletter at
troubador.co.uk/bookshop